Table of Contents

Hung out to Die

A Riel Brava Mystery

By donalee Moulton

Print ISBNs
Amazon Print 978-0-2286-2495-0
LSI Print 978-0-2286-2496-7
B&N Print 978-0-2286-2497-4

Dedication

*For my godmother, Val Aikens. A
lifetime of love. An eternity of gratitude.*

Prologue

It has been estimated that anywhere from four to twelve percent of chief executive officers are psychopaths.

I am one of them.

Chapter 1

It's 9:40. The weekly management meeting starts in 20 minutes. I'm right on time. I crave the solitude of an empty boardroom that awaits collective disagreements, vibrating cell phones, assorted bagels, and turf wars.

I'm Riel Brava, chief executive officer of the Canadian Cannabis Corp. It's my job to corral, calm, and commandeer the six other members of my company's executive team who will soon fill the chairs in this room. I do it well, primarily because I do it with detachment.

My MBA from Stanford and my law degree from Yale have honed my detachment skills. Being a diagnosed psychopath, however, is the firm foundation on which these skills are founded. I respect both: what I know and who I am.

The quiet time foreshadowing a meeting is planning time (thanks, Ivy league) and settling-in time (thanks, Dr. Roberta Coney, therapist). It is my alone time. I can breathe deeply, survey my domain, and steel my nerves. My files are alphabetized; the triple-spaced agenda is paper clipped to the top folder. I'm feeling in control. I'm content.

And then I'm not.

Norm's here. Norman Bedwell is our comptroller. Reliable, rumpled, risk averse. A stereotypical chartered accountant (except perhaps for the rumples). He shows up early when you include *There will be danishes* in the draft agenda.

And he wants to chat. Dear Lord.

Why do people feel this need to fill empty space, my empty space, with inconsequential tidbits about the weather, their health, or the latest on-the-job hiccup. Norm does not read me well. Despite my turned back, fingers rifling through files, and my complete lack of interest in the caterer's latest pastry, Norm persists.

"Gonna be a scorcher, eh, Riel?"

Truly, Norm, I don't give a shit. And what is a scorcher? I grew up in Santa Barbara, California. The record-breaking 22 degrees Celsius forecast for today in Elmsdale, Nova Scotia, where our cannabis production plant is located, means little to me. Literally. I must convert the damn Celsius to Fahrenheit (22 x 1.8 + 32). That's two seconds of my life I won't get back.

But I've learned how to play nicely, thanks to the Ivy League and Dr. Coney. "I do like it when the autumn thermostat tops 70 degrees," I say to Norm, a subtle reminder I am a come from away and proud of it. I smile and take my seat, pointedly glancing at my notes and not at Norm, who is devouring his third pastry. How is that possible?

I'm not sure if Norm will persist regardless of my averted eyes, but new opportunities have arisen. Susan Warrington, our director of human resources, has arrived and greets Norm like a long-lost friend, then reaches toward a danish. Instead, she stretches for the plate. Apparently, it's crooked.

Good grief.

"What are you planning for the Thanksgiving weekend?" she asks Norm, sounding almost conspiratorial, as if she honestly wants to know. I swear she giggled.

I lookup. *Is this feigned interest or genuine?* I'm always on the lookout for tips and techniques to fit in.

I understand the anticipation a long holiday weekend can engender, even if I don't feel it personally. Canadians celebrate Thanksgiving the second Monday of October, roughly six weeks before Americans. It's not as big an occasion as in the U.S., but it does serve as a harbinger of the long winter that invariably lies ahead, which makes the celebration more meaningful. Canadians serve up turkey, keep family close, and watch the Saskatchewan Roughriders trounce the Hamilton Tiger-Cats. *Don't ask. It's Canadian football. There are only three downs for frig's sake.*

Norm and Susan remain huddled in their pre-holiday conversation, and I'm hopeful I can block out their chitchat and focus on my opening remarks, a bit of banter delivered in a down-to-business tone. Those hopes are dashed with the early arrival of Lucy Chen, our chief compliance officer. A trim, no-nonsense woman with dark hair and eyes to match, Lucy stands apart from the rest of the team. Her job requires her to be arm's length, devil's advocate, and moral compass. She takes that role seriously. I've never heard Lucy giggle. She is the epitome of professional politeness though, and I can learn from this.

What I have learned today is that my pre-meeting plans go to hell when pastry is on the agenda.

Lucy smiles at her two colleagues, asks about their upcoming long weekend, and reaches for the last danish.

Chapter 2

It's an hour and 20 minutes before the sun is slated to appear over Grand Lake. With a hint of twilight in the air, the first frost of the season quietly nudges the horizon, and the Stanfield International Airport lights wink in the distance like an inside joke.

I'm showered, caffeinated, and ready to start the day. Early, of course, as the need for control is my second nature. As I climb out of the car, I tuck a cashmere scarf into my coat.

It's about 52 degrees, what Nova Scotians call ideal fall weather is 10 degrees chillier than a typical fall day in Santa Barbara. I'm dressed for the differential. I hurry across the near empty parking lot to escape the wind whisking leaves into whirlpools of red, brown, and yellow. I want to settle into my warm office and the day ahead.

The Canadian Cannabis Corp. (which everyone calls CCC) runs 24/7. Someone from security and grow ops is always onsite in case of a calamity or as a precaution against calamity. I'm not familiar with the night shift. Fact is, I don't know many of the frontline workers, regardless of when they work. Not my job. My HR director would disagree with that, I'm sure, but I've learned the road to leadership is not contingent on knowing everyone's name, rank, and serial number. Often a smile and a nod will do. I'm good at both. I've had years of practice.

I have my encrypted badge ready to scan with the radio-frequency identification reader. However, it appears the RFID security system isn't on. I feel something unpleasant tugging at my heart.

In a cannabis-production facility like ours, security is paramount. We have one million square feet of plants under production, pot after pot, row after row, and room after room. You don't want anyone walking out with your product at any stage of growth. Nor do you want unauthorized individuals to access your infrastructure, design, or facilities. So, if security is so important, why the hell am I looking at a friendly green light welcoming me inside without any preamble? Where the hell is the red light that forewarns the uninvited to the threat of motion detectors, alarm bells, and infrared sensors?

I breathe in for a count of four, hold for seven, and breathe out for a count of eight. It's a meditative technique that triggers the parasympathetic nervous system to activate the rest-and-digest response instead of the fight-or-flight reaction that is my natural tendency.

Heads will roll, or at least one will. I'll see to that. The first anniversary of legalized cannabis in Canada just passed, along with the recent Thanksgiving turkey and cranberry sauce. It's early days in the industry, and government regulators are watching companies like CCC closely. Every breach of protocol creates headlines. I am not a fan of headlines.

At our plant, there is one main gate through which all employees gain initial access by swiping a badge. The embedded code is read offsite by cloud-based security software that matches the data to an instantly uploaded photo of the person at the gate. Digital facial recognition immediately determines if there is at least a 98.7 percent match, and only then does someone gain access inside or outside the plant.

It takes three seconds.

At the moment, it takes even less. All you need to do is push on the door because it's open.

Once inside the first security check, people head in one of two directions. Left takes you to production and the heady aroma of green leaves turning into green cash. Right takes you to the administrative building, which is connected to the plant by a shared wall, but as required by law, there is no way to move from one building to the other without going outside. Whatever direction you turn, you'll face a second security protocol, a keypad passcode. These are updated every 12 hours, and employees are given access to an encrypted site to obtain the current code.

The passcode system is armed and waiting for me to enter a 13-letter-and-number sequence.

I'm in, and I am pissed. It's now 6:46 a.m. The plant will be in full swing in 44 minutes, but right now, it is in darkness except for the grow-op lights installed to benefit round-the-clock plant profusion. My three-storey admin building is also wrapped in darkness, at least from this angle, which raises the question: *How long has the damn security system been down*?

I'm moving full steam ahead up three flights of stairs to my office. Speed is not second nature to me. Given my innate state of being, caution is synonymous with survival. The faster you move, the more likely you are to misstep. Generally, that's something I can't risk.

I'm reaching for the hallway switch when I notice a light three doors down. That's Norm Bedwell's office. And that's unusual. Our comptroller is typically among the last to arrive. Only a fresh honey crueller from Tim Hortons has ever changed his timeline.

I'm running to Norm's office now, tirade at the ready. The only thing that can prevent the outside security system from working, aside from someone hacking into our server, is if the door doesn't latch firmly behind the entering employee. A loud audible click lets you know the system is armed, and then you can move forward. Employees are trained to wait for the click; if they don't, an alarm will sound for two minutes, albeit relatively soft as alarms go. But at this time of day, no one is around to hear it.

It must be Norm's fault, which may mean the system has only been down for minutes if he just arrived. It's a question I'm tossing at our comptroller even before I've stepped inside his office.

Norm doesn't answer.

He can't because he's swinging from a rope tossed over an open beam (the designer's brilliant idea), a noose tight around his neck. He's blue, but not as blue as I believe a dead man should look. This poses a dilemma. I need a few moments to assess my options and identify the safest and most effective course of action. However, I am aware I don't have the luxury of time. I've seen enough *Law and Order* episodes to know if you don't call the cops immediately, the delay in time will get noticed, and you're more likely to find yourself on the suspect list.

Dammit. I'm a suspect.

This realization hits at the same time I'm dialing 911. The perky young woman on the other end asks how she can help.

"I'm in the administrative office of the Canadian Cannabis Corp., and my comptroller appears to have hanged himself. He is dangling from a noose and turning blue."

"Sir, I have radioed for police; they are on their way," she says, inhaling to continue with her script.

I cut her off. "Look, I know I shouldn't disturb anything, but Norm may be alive. I'm going to grab his legs, so the noose doesn't cut into his windpipe."

Great, now she knows I understand how hanging kills someone.

It doesn't matter. I'm going to reduce the pressure around Norm's neck. His feet are tucked into the crease in my left arm, his testicles on par with my bottom lip. I'm not a small man, 6'2", and I work out regularly, so I can maintain this, albeit a distasteful posture, for quite some time.

I hear sirens, and it hits me. The police won't gain access to the building without destroying expensive technology. I explain this to the 911 operator. She is not that interested in the cost of our tech.

"I'm going to get someone to open the gate for the police," I tell her. "That means I'll have to hang up. I'm on the third floor of the admin building, inside the only office with a light on. My name is Riel Brava. I'm the CEO."

I end the call, rapidly going through the list of 47 employees that work for the company to find those I know. Only senior managers are apt to be in this building, and Michael Graves, head of our legal department (indeed, he makes up the entire legal department), is likely to be at his desk. He's ambitious, comes from private practice where 60-hour weeks are the norm, and has a baby daughter who gets up at 5 a.m. with a distinctive and lengthy wail. I'm told nothing will drive you to the office faster.

I dial his extension.

Michael answers.

"Michael, I don't have time to explain, but the police are on their way. Please meet them at the front gate and bring them to Norm Bedwell's office. And hurry."

I like to think I could hear his feet pounding one floor below, but the walls, even in the admin building, are very well insulated. The truth is flowering cannabis stinks, and we've gone to great lengths to keep our facility and the nearby community odour free. The last thing we want is disgruntled neighbors.

I'm straining to hear what is happening outside, but without any luck. *So, the contractors did use expensive insulation.* I attempt counting, another meditative technique, but also a way to estimate when police should be here. It takes only a few minutes, I hope.

The next thing I remember is someone tapping my shoulder.

"Sir, you can let go," a uniformed officer says. He looks like a high school student who should be in a t-shirt and jeans, sneaking beer into a dance. Surely, too young for law enforcement and certainly too young to be in charge. I loosen my grip, and Norm's testicles inch closer to my lower lip.

"I've got him," the officer says, then pries Norm loose from my elbow socket. He sounds thoughtful or compassionate, and I am uncertain why.

Of course. *Norm is dead.*

* * *

I'm back at my office doorway, attempting to find some order in the chaos that has become my morning. I take solace in the familiar surroundings. The Yawkey reversible desk in tempered glass and white gloss reassures me. The spiral-shaped desk lamp reaffirms that what goes around comes around. The small, neat stack of file folders is where it belongs to the right of the laptop. I breathe easily here.

Before I take a second breath and the first step into the office proper, I sense company. Marcia, my executive assistant, is hovering. Marcia, unfathomably pronounced

"Marsh-a," is not generally a fusser, but I guess death trumps normalcy. Usually, I'd chafe at this behaviour; right now, I'm too removed from what's happening around me. I need to figure out what's going on inside me.

Stephen King, Anne Rice, Alfred Hitchcock, and their literary ilk portray psychopaths, also often called sociopaths, as evil, demented, and violent. Yawn. We are indifferent to many human emotions unless they benefit us directly. But for most of us – and there are a lot of us – we prefer to be left alone to earn our way, enjoy our own company, and embrace anything but the human condition. We're pretty good at letting you think we're one of you when we're nothing like you at all.

When shit hits the fan, or someone throws a rope over a beam and dangles at the end of it, the stakes go up. Way up. The margin for error increases significantly. I can get through most days with relative ease. I've learned to read faces, voice cues, and body language. I know when I'm on terra firma and about to step into quicksand. Norm's death is undoubtedly a quagmire. I have few reference points and no clear understanding of the process or what steps to take next. I do not appreciate getting hung out to die.

I'm sitting at my desk sipping some syrupy soy latte pumpkin-spice thing. My employees do not appreciate the fine art of the coffee bean, and Marcia is absently shuffling papers like her presence makes a difference. Perhaps it does. Perhaps my discomfort will be considered as concern or even compassion. Who knows, I might get through this thing unscathed.

It takes 6 minutes and 42 seconds for a uniformed officer to frame my doorway. It took roughly the same amount of time for the first four officers to arrive at our front gate and thunder their way upstairs. They asked me, each of them at some point, to wait in my office while they investigated. Not an optional request, and here I dutifully sit in apparent distress. Meanwhile, my mind is firing on all cylinders.

"Sorry to interrupt," says the police officer.

He is not one of the quartet from Norm's office. This man is older, maybe early 40s, carrying a small notebook. I can't believe they still use paper. Then I'm shocked I can think about something so inane as paper.

"Please come in." I gesture in what I hope is a warm yet distracted manner toward the chair in front of my desk. As long as I focus, I should be fine.

"I have a few questions about," he glances at his notepad, "Mr. Bedwell."

"I'd like to help," I respond, "but Norm and I weren't close." Hopefully, that gives me distance from what happened and any expectations that I can be helpful, even though I lean forward to demonstrate my willingness to assist.

The officer asks me about Norm's job at Canadian Cannabis, his home life (like I know) and, as he puts it, "the events of this morning." I walk the officer through my morning, starting at 6:46 until the extrication of Norm's testicles from the vicinity of my mouth.

I catch the look on the officer's face. It's unclear what I've done wrong. His smile is almost friendly. "You arrived at 6:46. That's pretty specific."

Ahh, this I can explain. "I will admit I'm anal," I say, grinning somewhat, "but in this case, I specifically noted the time because the security alarm wasn't on. That's information we'll need for our review."

I have jolted the officer, and he's not hiding it. He looks up quickly from his notepad. "The alarm was off?"

I confirm the green "unarmed" light was on and the door was open. "Do you think Norm was so upset he forgot to lock it behind him?" I'm thinking out loud now, something I make a point not to do, but I'm off-guard.

The seasoned officer appears like my question is familiar territory. "The investigation is ongoing, and every detail helps." He hesitates, uncertainty perhaps, or is this thoughtfulness? "Are you surprised," he looks down at his notes again, "Mr. Bedwell killed himself."

Dammit Norm. Suicide, really? Clearly my astonishment is on display for the world to see.

"I'm sorry, sir," the officer says. "I understand this is distressing."

If Norm were alive, I'd kill him myself. This is not a comfortable spot for me: winging it. I take my time. "It's the word 'suicide.' I haven't said it, even to myself, until now."

That's good. Right? The officer asks again if I'm surprised Norm took his own life. This is a new-for-me experience, and I answer truthfully. "I don't know. Yesterday, I would have said Norm was his old self, nothing unusual. Today, I'm reliving every conversation, every hello in the hallway."

"Not to worry, sir." The officer rises out of his chair. "Suicides often hide their intent from everyone."

"Thank you."

The officer smiles kindly.

Yes, I said exactly the right thing.

* * *

Remember the security issue and the government's scrutiny on what happens in the cannabis industry. Well, that potential scrutiny also applies when someone commits suicide in a production facility.

As CEO, I understand what is expected of me when something unexpected hits the fan. I don't shy away from difficult situations or conversations. I'm aiming, someday soon, to run for a political office, perhaps the highest political office in the U.S., and making tough decisions comes with the territory. I roll up my sleeves, literally, and reach for the phone.

My first call is to David Clements, our contact at the Department of Justice, the federal regulator for cannabis production. I get a voicemail. I leave a nuanced message asking David to get in touch with me as soon as possible. I'm very good at nuance.

My second call is to our HR director, Susan Warrington. She is in my office within two minutes.

She must have sprinted.

Susan is dependable and looks it with her bob-cut hair that is functional not fashionable. She invariably wears a suit in one of her two favorite colours: grey or slate. Her shoes have a small heel, which is practical and professional. As her job title would indicate, Susan is a good listener and takes all things HR very seriously.

"This is dreadful," she says, sounding like she means it.

It's certainly inconvenient, I think, and it will require a mountain of paperwork, but "dreadful?" Not so much. Then I realize she thinks it's dreadful because Norm is dead. I nod sympathetically, a slight movement of the head, eyes downcast.

Susan continues going on about how awful this whole situation is. Frankly, I'm a little bewildered. The 5'4" silver-haired woman who seemingly runs HR with a wave of her hand did not strike me as someone who would wobble at the death of a colleague, especially Norm. As far as I knew, they were not close. But perhaps this is what suicide does to people. I'll watch others in the office to monitor their responses. And I must remember to call it a "tragedy."

Within 10 minutes, Susan and I devise a plan to inform the staff and investors. We'll develop preliminary Q&As in case of media calls. These also will come in handy for any internal or external discussion of what happened, even with the police.

By the time we're through, it's decided Susan will meet with Lucy Chen, our chief compliance officer, to go over the game plan, and legal will prepare a summary of potential issues, pressing or otherwise. It occurs to me Norm's family could sue us. For what? I don't know. That will be up to legal to determine. I add to my to-do list, "find out if Norm has a family."

I look at Susan, who should know. She's HR. "I would like to reach out to Norm's family," I say. "Do you have contact information for them?"

Clearly, I've disconcerted Susan again with the mention of family. Tough.

I'm CEO of the largest cannabis production facility in Atlantic Canada. I'll be expected to act sympathetic and yet, available.

"I'll get that to you," says Susan. "This will be so hard on his son, Bran."

"Like the 'muffin?'" I wonder, then realize I've wondered aloud.

"No," Susan says, "like Bran Stark."

Bran Stark from *Game of Thrones*. Norm, you are full of surprises today.

* * *

Susan barely sets foot outside my office door when Marcia steps inside. It's going to be one of those days. Marcia wears her "Oh dear" face as she says, "You have a call on your private line. It's the senator."

Oh dear. Senator John Williams is the majority owner of Canadian Cannabis, although you won't find any obvious paper trail documenting that ownership. John is far too business savvy for that. He's also too politically savvy to get involved in the day-to-day operations of a marijuana company based in another country. I'm assuming suicide falls outside day-to-day operations.

I have no idea how John knows about Norm, but this is not unusual. John Williams is a powerful man with powerful connections, and he has learned that even the most innocuous issue can become media fodder. Most of the time, I'm left on my own to run CCC as I see fit. We have monthly recap meetings, and I know the senator is only a phone call away if the need arises. Until now, the need has not arisen.

John doesn't waste time on small talk. "What the hell is going on up there?"

"To be honest, that isn't a question I have an answer to now," I say. Truthfully. "There's been a death on the premises. Apparent suicide. The police are conducting their investigation."

"Did you know this fellow?" John's usually well-modulated voice is now closer to a bark, and I can sense his annoyance and maybe a touch of fear. Anything that can potentially derail the senator's political ambitions quickly takes the edge off his charm.

"Norm Bedwell is our comptroller… was our comptroller," I say, instinctively correcting my grammar. "I saw him every day in the office, but I didn't know him well."

John snorts. I'm unsure if this is derisive, as he knows I'm not close to many people. Well, no one, in fact. It may also have been a grunt of begrudging pride. Keep your distance, and people can't take you down.

Before John can make another guttural sound, I assure him it's business as usual, and I have reached out to the regulator to affirm there is no cause for concern.

"Have you contacted the family?" the senator asks a little more calmly.

I hesitate. It's almost like I can feel John tensing on the other end of the line.

"You call that family now. Tonight, you get your ass over there."

It's advice I'll heed. John Williams knows how to win friends and influence people. It's a political necessity, and I need to be adept at it if I'm going to be president of the United States someday. And I am.

Before I can respond, John hangs up. His final words are, "Tell Tiffany I love her."

Tiffany is John's daughter and my wife. John does love her. I, naturally, don't.

* * *

Marcia is somehow back in my office. It's like she's an apparition, a lanky, grey-haired apparition with a note. It's the contact info for Norm's family. Warrington has come through with precision and speed, as usual. Not only do I have an alphabetical list of names and biographical information, but I also have a photo to go with each name. Got to give it to Warrington; she is highly organized.

Marcia informs me the police have officially contacted Norm's family, and I can reach out whenever I want.

As I'm slowly dialing the 10 digits, I'm also slowly mapping out my game plan or trying to. Sure, I've been to hospitals and funerals before. I know the standard behaviour protocols for such grievous occasions. But I have never taken center stage at these events.

The phone rings then a woman answers. She sounds okay.

"I'm looking for Faye Bedwell," I say. "It's Riel Brava. I'm CEO of Canadian Cannabis."

There is the briefest pause, and a soft voice says, "I'm Faye's sister-in-law, Samantha. Let me get her for you."

The woman who comes back on the line does not sound okay. Her voice is shaky and fragile. I envision a woman escorted to the phone and then reaching tentatively for the receiver.

"Faye, this is Riel." I'm sure we've met on previous occasions, although I cannot picture this woman for the life of me. I should have checked out her photo more closely before I dialed.

"Thank you for calling."

God Canadians are polite, and Nova Scotians may be the politest of them all. But I can also do polite. "Faye, please accept my heartfelt sympathy. Norm was a special man, and he holds a special place in our hearts," I say, somewhat proud of myself.

I looked up condolence notes on the internet while waiting for Faye to come to the phone. This was the second note on the list. I like it.

So does Faye. "Thank you for that. It's nice to hear."

"I can't imagine what you're going through." I continue reading from my script. "We are all here for you and Bran. Please, if there is anything I can do, let me know."

The tears are flowing now. Faye mumbles something as the line goes dead in my hand.

I smile. Obviously, I handled that well.

* * *

My day is turning around. The call with the family went smoothly, and so did my following conversation, this one with the regulator. I calmly explain the situation to David Clements, making it sound exactly like what it is, an unfortunate circumstance but not a crisis.

David concurs. "Sorry, you are all having to go through this."

I believe he means it.

"Be aware the media may call," he cautions. "Keep me posted if they do."

And that was that. Compliance completed. Justice served.

The idea of media involvement is a bit disconcerting, but suicides are not usually covered on the six o'clock news. I remain hopeful the trend is not about to reverse itself.

* * *

Tiffany is waiting for me when I walk in the door around 6:30. My wife is head-turning gorgeous. She's 5'7", naturally blonde, green-eyed, athletically lean, and simultaneously curvaceous.

She could be a model. In fact, she has been. When I met her, she modeled for IMG and made a name for herself. It turned out, a name she didn't want.

Tiffany knows she is stunning; she just doesn't care. Fame is not what she craves. Family is.

"You okay?" Tiffany asks as I hang up my coat.

"I'm reeling," I say, maybe even meaning it.

Tiffany hands me a gin and tonic, already poured and at the ready. She must have heard me pull into the garage. "Of course, you're reeling. These situations are hard for anyone, but especially for you."

I look up, eyebrows raised, on edge now. Where's Tiffany going with her last comment?

She catches my confusion. "You don't do well with showing sympathy. You're more comfortable removed from the crowd."

31

Evidently a day of curiosities. Who knew Tiffany had this in her: observational skills and behavioural analysis? God, I hope this is a one-off. Even as I think this, somewhat snarkily (it has been a trying day), I know I am being unfair to Tiffany, the daughter of a firmly entrenched, always-re-elected U.S. senator. She has been on display since wiggling out of her mother's womb. She knows how to read a room and how to read a face. Been reading mine for 10 years, and I rely on her insight and acumen when it comes to doing and saying the right thing.

I married Tiffany because she is the daughter of Senator John Williams. Like her name – why would anyone do that to a child? Might as well have called her "Lamp" – Tiffany is light, airy. Biblically "Tiffany" means "manifestation of god." Today, the name given to thousands of white girls with blond hair and blue eyes means "manifestation of whimsy."

My wife asks for little. She knows my political aspirations and the role of the political wife. She signed on for both when we married. Even so, she expects a relationship, including intimacy. Lord, spare me.

Tonight, I'm given a reprieve. I'm grieving. Tiffany takes my silence for confirmation of her concern and assumes my stare is one of admiration and love. And we're back to familiar ground.

"Do you want to change?"

My confusion shows. Again.

"We have to go to the Bedwells."

Crap, she has talked to her father. A shower would give me time to think and plan. It would also give me time to fret. I opt to ruminate in the car on the way over.

* * *

Tiffany must have called Faye Bedwell to let her know we were coming. The grieving widow greets us at the front door. She's a mess. Her hair is tousled, her eyes red, and her face blotchy. She waves us inside. "Thank you for coming."

Tiffany leans in and hugs her. "We are here for you." The widow weeps. I closely continue to watch how my wife does this. I am always amazed at the ease and naturalness with which Tiffany draws people to her and makes them feel comfortable.

From a bag I didn't even realize Tiffany had in her hand, she removes a lasagna she purchased from our favorite Italian restaurant. "A little comfort food," she says, leaning in again. I suspect the touching is likely to go on for a while.

Another woman enters the fray, takes the lasagna, and leads us into the living room. Several people are there, including a child I assume must be Muffin. Dammit, Bran.

I sit down uncomfortably and realize everybody is looking just as uncomfortable. I relax. Tiffany mingles, doing it well. People are responding to her. Perhaps she should run for president. Ha, who knew I had a sense of humor.

I don't know who these people are, but they all seem to know their surroundings and the Bedwell family. I assume they are relatives and neighbours. I'll confirm that with Tiffany.

I glance at my watch in what I hope is a nonchalant move. This is a perfunctory visit; I'm hoping we're in and out in under 30 minutes.

As I look up, I realize Muffin is looking directly at me. Dammit. Bran. I'm hoping he didn't see my sidelong glance. I smile. It's a mixture of warmth and sadness. I get a quivery smile in return. This is good. The kid must not know what looking at a watch indicates. I'm in the clear.

Tiffany catches my eye and motions me toward the kitchen. As always, protocol is her forte. I rise and follow her to the adjoining room. It's warm from the oven and stove, brightly lit, and HGTV comfortable. I struggle to picture Norm here eating, doing dishes, or sipping coffee. I fail. The fact is, I don't even know if Norm drank coffee. All I seem to know for certain is his fondness for pastry.

Samantha, Norm's sister, sets our lasagna on a table laden with more lasagna, rolls, salads, soups, and sandwiches. She sees me staring. "People have been kind."

"As they should. How is Bran doing?" I realize it's a stupid question, but commonly asked in situations like this.

"He's shaken. And confused." Samantha turns, a little uncertainly, I think. Now she looks me in the eye.

Oh, god.

"Can I ask you something?"

I want to point out that she already has asked me something, but I know that would not be appropriate. I nod.

"Did you know Norm well?"

The real answer is, "Well enough to keep him at arm's length and out of my life." The suitable answer is more nuanced. Hesitation works well in these situations, I've discovered. Psychologists and shrinks like to use indicators like this to demonstrate the presence of psychopathy or sociopathy. It doesn't always. A delay is acceptable and anticipated for real people grappling to find the appropriate words.

My history with Norm is short. Canadian Cannabis opened in 2015, producing medical marijuana for a global market of patients suffering everything from depression to fibromyalgia to cancer. I arrived 18 months later to prepare the company for the domestic recreational cannabis market as Canada became only the second country in the world to legalize marijuana.

Norm was already in place when I assumed the helm. I got the feeling he would have liked to have been friends, which is the last thing I ever wanted. Distance is a safety valve for me. Get too close, and you are more likely to trip up. In Norm's case, it was also chemistry. I don't have friends, but I understand the concept. You must have common ground, mutual respect, and a shared fondness for each other. We didn't have that. More accurately, I didn't have that.

I look up at Samantha. "I've known Norm since I moved here three years ago. I saw him almost every day. We worked well together, but we were not close." It's an honest answer. Shit. Where did that come from?

"Did you expect this?" Samantha asks.

More confusion on my part.

"That he killed himself," she explains somewhat cautiously.

It's a great question. The obvious answer is "Yes." I dig a little deeper. The answer is the same: "Yes." That's what I tell Samantha.

"Me too." Norm's sister twists a dish towel in her hands tighter and tighter. "I keep going over it in my head. It just doesn't make sense."

I remain silent. I've learned people will fill the silence, doing the work for me.

"I'm down from Sydney because Norm and Faye were supposed to be going to Cuba for a week's vacation, a romantic getaway. I was staying with Bran. They had non-refundable tickets. They had plans."

I agree it doesn't make sense.

"Do you think he killed himself?"

My bewilderment is obvious even to me. I feel the shockwaves in my bones. "What else could it be?" I simply did not see this question coming even in the long list of possibilities I reviewed on the drive over.

"I don't know," Samantha says, looking me directly in the eye. "But I don't believe my brother killed himself."

It turns out Samantha's disbelief was well-founded.

Chapter 3

Today is Friday, October 16th. It's been 48 hours since Norm said hasta la vista to this world. I believe things should be back to normal by now. I am wrong.

Marcia arrives promptly at 8:30. I hear the gentle whirlwind of activity as she settles in with her Starbucks decaf mocha latte, a morning tradition, and begins tapping something on her ergonomically approved keyboard.

I relax.

That is my first mistake of the day. Ten minutes later, Marcia is in my doorway. It's as if she glides on air.

"There's a detective from the Halifax Police Department here to see you." The pitch of her voice is up at least one octave. I can't tell if this is nervousness or excitement. I make a mental note to work on distinguishing those emotions.

The man now striding uninvited into my office is a fine specimen. I'd estimate 6'3", ebony skin, broad shoulders, slim waist, with biceps evident but not bulging. "Sorry to interrupt." He smiles and hands me a plain white business card.

The card is as basic as the paper it is printed on. In addition to a phone number, there is nothing on it but his name, Sergeant Lin Raynes. I hesitate at the "Lin." Not a name I am familiar with, although there are many names that you'll hear in Nova Scotia you are unlikely to hear elsewhere. Breton, Ainslie, Xavier, Burpee. But "Lin" is a first for me.

Not surprisingly, the detective sees me pause as I stare at his card. I get another smile. "Short for Franklin. My mother was adamant no one was going to call me Frankie."

"I like your mother. I'm Riel Garcia. Riel is short for Gabriel. When I was in grade one, some kid sitting behind me called me Gabe. I went home that afternoon and informed my mother I wanted to be called Riel. From that point on, I was." I'm disconcerted by my candor. Sharing stories with strangers is not second nature to me.

I bring the conversation back to business and my comfort zone. "How can I help you?"

"We have some follow-up questions. Do you have a few minutes?"

"Please sit." I motion to the black Belanger bonded leather chair in front of my desk. The seat is firm but padded. It's cushioned and curved with no angles to dig into calves or shins. In hindsight, I wonder if

I've made it too inviting for people to linger in my office.

Raynes moves with the ease of someone comfortable with people and comfortable in his body. He's athletic and aware of the impression he makes on people. I am not fooled. The burgundy mock neck sweater is cashmere, and the tan chinos are tailored to fit. Raynes may appear as if he grabs clothes from a pile on the floor, but this outfit required thought and effort. I know because it's how I get dressed every morning.

The detective attempts to reassure me I'm not in trouble, so I am, naturally, on full alert. "Just a few loose ends to tie up. All routine." The smile is back. "Were you close with Mr. Bedwell?" It's intended to be an offhand comment. It's anything but.

I breathe a little easier. It's a question I can answer honestly. "We worked together for three years. But we didn't spend any time socializing. I'm afraid I won't be any help on that front."

"Do you know if anyone was close to him?"

I hesitate. This time it's not nervousness. It's me thinking. "Susan Warrington is our director of human resources. She will be better able to answer that question. Would you like me to call her?"

"In a minute. First, walk me through yesterday." Before I can speak, and as if he's heard this a thousand times, the detective adds with his crooked smile, "I know you've told the police constable this already, but I need to hear it firsthand."

I tell Raynes what I told the young officer yesterday. He seems interested in the security problem at the front gate.

"Is that unusual?"

"It better damn well be," I respond without filtering the thought first.

Raynes seems to appreciate the honesty and the promptness of my reply. He smiles.

"As you know, cannabis is a new industry in Canada. We're under constant scrutiny. We go out of our way to ensure our security measures are advanced and operational. Obviously, we failed yesterday." I return the smile.

"So, what happened yesterday?"

I'm not sure how to interpret the detective's question.

He catches my uncertainty. "Why was the security system disabled?"

"You think it was deliberately disabled?" Now I'm catching him off guard.

"I'm wondering why the system wasn't working yesterday."

I sigh. "That is the million-dollar question. I spoke with Neela Khoury, our director of IT, and she's investigating, albeit nervously. IT is her domain; if anything hits the fan, it will land on her."

"Do you mind if we call her in here?"

This is important. As if on cue, Marcia appears in the doorway. A few minutes later, a somewhat breathless Neela is in my office, shaking hands with Raynes. And I didn't think she could get more nervous than at our last meeting, about the IT budget.

Neela reminds me of a crane. She is tall and slender with long legs and fine black hair. And like an ibis, Neela flutters. I always feel she is itching to take flight. She is new to the cannabis sector and new to Nova Scotia. The 27-year-old tech whiz moved here from Chennai, India, with her parents more than a decade ago. She has one foot in her new world, one foot in another world, and is at home in neither. I can identify.

Raynes asks about the security system.

Neela launches into a soliloquy about tamper switches, remote junction boxes, and disconnection protocols.

Raynes is as confused as I am. "What do you think went wrong?" he asks.

I think he's being solicitous.

"I think someone turned the system off," Neela says.

"You can just turn the damn system off?" I realize my voice has risen, and I'm unsure if Raynes is startled or covering up a grin.

"With the right security clearance, you can. We do this when large pieces of equipment or new seeds arrive. It speeds up getting things from the parking lot to the plant. But it is always overseen by a senior member of the team and immediately turned back on to full capacity," Neela says quickly as if anticipating my next question or a strenuous objection.

"How could someone turn it off?" Raynes asks with a voice much softer than mine had been.

"You need the access code," Neela continues without missing a beat. "A total of 10 employees have this code, seven senior managers and three plant supervisors, one for each shift." Our plant runs 24/7 because plants grow 24/7, and there needs to be someone who knows what they're doing on site for each shift. That might change in the future when grow-ops become mainstream, and Canadians become convinced the end of the world is not linked to the legalization of cannabis. But for now, it's all hands on deck.

"Can you tell…." Raynes and I both start to ask the same question.

Neela doesn't need us to finish it. "Norm turned off the system at 5:02 am on Wednesday."

* * *

I wonder if my face looks agape like Raynes's face. Why the hell would Norm turn off the security system? I strive to put that information in the context of his death. Does it make it easier to commit suicide? Is it quieter? Is it a last act of defiance?

Security systems are turned off to unload heavy equipment and delicate plants. I realize Raynes is probing the same ground, nudging Neela for possible reasons. She seems confused. It's beyond her expertise. And mine.

"Here is a list of people who signed in to the plant on Wednesday before the system was disconnected," she says, handing it to me.

I take the list of seven names and recognize five. The other two are likely plant workers.

Raynes asks for a copy. Marcia magically appears to take the list from my hand for copying.

"Could anyone have used Mr. Bedwell's access code?" Raynes asks.

Neela looks puzzled. "Only Norm would know his access information, and he would never share that," she says as if the detective has just inquired about the number of unicorns we employ.

Raynes doesn't seem bothered by the erroneous conviction that we all protect our passwords or the IT director's perceptible belief that his last question was absurd. He thanks Neela. I notice his hand resting on her shoulder briefly. He's being solicitous. I must remember that move for future situations where I hold power but want to appear approachable. That's most situations.

I stand, my way of indicating the interview is at an end. Raynes remains seated, so a situation where power does not swing my way. The detective is comfortable with his authority. "You mentioned your HR director," he says.

Of course. "Susan Warrington. Marcia can take you down to her office."

"Would you mind if we met here?" Raynes offers no explanation for his request, and my brain hurts from struggling to figure out what the fuck is going on.

I shrug my agreement and then walk to the door. I ask Marcia to get Susan. The two women must have sprinted because the HR director comes through the door before I settle back into my chair.

"You wanted to see me?" Susan asks, looking in any direction but at Raynes. She adjusts a file on my desk that is an inch over the edge.

Raynes stands up and introduces himself. It's all very comfortable and casual. I'll have to dissect how he does that.

Susan relaxes. It's an unusual state for our HR director. She is always on edge, waiting to pounce on some potential human resources violation or oversight. The 5' 3" director may seem like a modern-day grandmother, who likes nothing more than baking cookies with the little ones in her life, but she sees her role more as that of a superhero, sans cape, defending staff rights. She can be a pain in the ass.

"How can I help?" Susan believes she is taking charge.

"I'm wondering if you can tell me a bit about Mr. Bedwell?"

Susan is on familiar ground now. HR is her wheelhouse, and she makes an effort to connect with all employees. Hell, I have even heard her giggle when talking with Norm. Susan starts with Norm's professional bio. He graduated from Dalhousie University in 2000, got his CPA in 2004, and worked for the provincial government, first health, then the government-owned liquor corporation for 11 years before joining CCC in 2015.

As Susan recites Norm's job description, Raynes cuts her off, with a smile, naturally. It must be genetic. "This is very helpful."

I swear Susan swooned.

Raynes continues, "I was wondering, though, if you could tell me more about Mr. Bedwell, the man, the co-worker, the husband."

The request seems to take Susan aback. Now, I discretely smile. I can't determine why Susan has suddenly lost her footing, but I am enjoying the moment. "What would you like to know?"

"I want to know about him. Did he get on well with colleagues? Was he liked by the staff? Any close friends here at work?"

I'm a little baffled where Raynes is taking this. Uncertain if he's setting a trap or off his game.

Susan is no longer swooning. "That is not something I would be privy to as director of HR." The edge in her voice surprises me. I hate surprises.

Either Raynes doesn't hear it, or it doesn't faze him. "I'd never ask you to share private information," he says, seemingly understanding the source of her resistance. "As an observant woman and capable HR director, I would appreciate any insight you might have into Norm's personality and his presence here."

The son of a bitch is smooth, successfully so.

"I can tell you we've had no complaints from colleagues or direct reports about Norm. He certainly seemed well-liked, and the corporation valued his work. Wouldn't you agree?" Susan looks directly at me.

Now it's my turn for discomfort. Raynes isn't smiling. His eyes meet mine, and I opt for honesty. "As I've said, I didn't know Norm well on a personal level. Certainly, he was agreeable, easy to get along with, and helpful. But what he loved about his job or thought about the people he worked with I don't know." But I wondered if I should have. I'll ask Tiffany.

* * *

Raynes is standing now, picking up his coat. "Thank you for your time. Sorry to intrude."

"I hope it was helpful. I'm sorry I didn't have more to tell you about Norm."

"We're just tying up a few loose ends," Raynes says anticipating my unspoken question. On cue, Marcia glides in with the copy of the employees who had signed in early on the day Norm died.

"Thank you." The smile is back. "Did you know Mr. Bedwell?"

* * *

I should have known Marcia would be the most well-informed of anyone in the office. I mean, when you can meld into the shadows, you see what others miss.

Marcia glances at me to be sure it is okay to speak openly. "Norm was one of the good ones. He genuinely liked people and liked to connect. That said, he was a bit of a numbers' nerd and not the best conversationalist. People often invented meetings or made a quick exit when they saw him coming."

I'm impressed, and so is Raynes. I am embarrassed. Marcia is right. In hindsight, I could have come up with this information.

Raynes looks pleased, it's the info he wanted. His smile might be genuine. "How was his home life?"

Marcia has a perceptible moment of indecision, then says, "We don't have a lot of work events with family." She avoids my eyes. "I do know Norm talked to Faye and Bran everyday. He'd text her when he was leaving for home, so she'd know when to expect him."

"That's nice."

"He was nice." There is an edge to Marcia's voice. "Fact is, he was milquetoast. No one would want to hurt him."

Of course, no one would want to hurt him. What an absurd thing to say.

It took me a few seconds, much longer than it had taken Marcia, to figure out. Why was a Halifax Regional Police detective standing in my office, asking questions nicely and smiling indiscriminately?

The cops don't believe Norm Bedwell killed himself.

Sonofabitch.

* * *

Raynes is in his element now, and apparently, so is Marcia. I remain in left field waiting for the ball to drop.

"Why do you think Mr. Bedwell would kill himself? It sounds like he was content,"

49

Raynes says. The gauntlet, albeit a polite, smiling gauntlet, has been thrown.

Marcia picks it up deftly and tosses it back. "You need to speak to someone who knew him much better than me."

Raynes doesn't miss a beat. "Who would that be?"

Marcia looks him straight in the eye. "Susan Warrington."

* * *

The director of HR is back in my office. She doesn't want to be here. Neither do I. Raynes apologizes for the return visit. Susan isn't buying the candy-coating this time. "I'm unsure what more I can do," she says before the police detective can get a word in edgewise.

"It's come to our attention," he says, looking my way, "that you may have been closer to Mr. Bedwell than many others here."

"So?" Nice response, I think.

Raynes doesn't agree. "I don't mean to put you in an awkward position here, but we are trying to determine exactly what happened to Mr. Bedwell and why. We'd appreciate your help."

Susan seems to wilt a little. "What do you want to know?"

"Who would want to hurt Mr. Bedwell?" There is no preamble; there is no smile.

Susan responds in kind. "No one."

"Everyone liked him?" Raynes asks with a hint of skepticism.

"No," Susan says with a dash of disdain, "but no one hated him."

That seems to set Raynes back. Maybe it was her tone or the accuracy of her assessment. He opts for a different tack. "How do you know?"

"As HR director, I spend a lot of time with the senior managers, including Norm. I get to know them. Sometimes we work late hours, share a meal, or share pleasantries."

Did I know this? Maybe.

"There's nothing else you can think of that we should know about Mr. Bedwell?" The relief on Susan's face is palpable, but before she can answer, Raynes continues, "or his family?"

Susan takes a long breath. "His son, Bran, was being bullied physically at school and on social media." Her face tightens. "It's nasty."

I don't know what Raynes heard or saw that I missed, but this hit the mark.

"Norm was beside himself," Susan adds. "He asked for advice about how to handle such situations."

"What did you tell him?" Raynes asks.

"The usual. Address the problem head on. Meet with the other boy's parents to discuss the situation. Talk to the school principal and the guidance counsellor."

"Did it work?" Raynes wants to know.

"You'll have to check with Faye, but I think it's safe to say the traditional avenues to resolve issues like Bran's did not work. Norm was suing the family and the school for cyberbullying."

Canada is not a litigious country, at least compared to the U.S. Parents suing other parents would be a big deal here.

Cyberbullying is also a hot-button issue, especially in Nova Scotia. The province was the first in the country to pass cyberbullying legislation following the suicide of a 17-year-old girl who had digital photos taken of her during a sexual assault and then posted online. While most people admired the government's motivation, the law didn't stand up in court. It had to be rewritten but is now back in force. Norm's case would make headlines.

I suspect Raynes knows all this and the pain bullying can cause parents. It looks like he has found someone who didn't like Norm Bedwell and also found a motive.

Now maybe I can have my office back.

* * *

I don't deal well with discomfort. First, it's an unusual emotion for me. While I'm always on tenterhooks, I'm also generally confident I can handle what comes my way. That confidence is in part the natural assurance that comes with being 6'2", 165 pounds, with black hair, a chiseled chin, a 35" waist, and good looks (if I say so myself). It's also part experience. When empathy is not coded in your DNA, you quickly learn to observe the world around you in ongoing detail.

Second, I understand the repercussions of standing apart from the crowd. For most people, misreading the room, misunderstanding a spoken implication, or misinterpreting a stolen glance, is, at most, embarrassing. For me, it's life-threatening. Despite the social media embrace of all things mental health, the reality is most people are not comfortable with or accepting of people who do not think and act like them. That's me, and my goal is to be president of the United States of America someday. *Elect America's first psychopath* is not a winning slogan. Chances are it's not even accurate.

The whole week has been a shit show for me. My natural rhythm is off, my usually sanguine laugh is forced, and my response time is slow. I fear it's about to get worse. According to the list Neela gave Raynes and me, seven people signed in before the security system shut off at 5:02 a.m. But when I arrived at 6:46, eight cars were in the parking lot. I know this because I counted them.

Surveying the landscape is as natural to me as breathing. It helps me to prepare for what lies ahead. Counting cars in our parking lot, in the early and late hours helps me know how many people I'm likely to confront, run into, or need to go out of my way to avoid. There were eight cars. Either someone didn't sign in or they left their car in the lot overnight. Chances are it's door number one.

The issue for me is what I do with this information. I don't want to embed myself any further in this matter. I am not Columbo. I'm an adept and effective CEO. I'm a lawyer whose training is to avoid risk, and I'm presidential material with a career path intended to get me there in the next decade or so.

Every fibre in my being tells me to keep this information to myself and keep my head down. It will go away. After all, Norm is dead, and nothing we do will change that. It's not about right and wrong for me but about convenience and protection. If I tell Raynes, I'll seem honest and, indeed, will be honest. That, at least, could not come back to bite me in the ass. But who wants to be the idiot who counts cars in a parking lot?

It seriously is not my week. I know what I need to do. Ask Tiffany.

* * *

My wife yells, "I'm in the kitchen," before I even have my shoes off. When I look up, she's standing in front of me, smiling. Her shoulder-length blonde hair is swept back in a ponytail, and she is wearing her let's-relax attire, fashionably stressed jeans and an East Coast Lifestyle t-shirt with long purple sleeves.

"Dinner's about an hour away. Moussaka."

To many, the word "moussaka" implies the presence of meat. Not to Tiffany. She has embraced the new Canada Food Guide as a religious treatise. The damn guide is pushing for a 50 percent plant-based diet. I am not a fan.

An hour, however, gives me time to broach the delicate issue of honesty with the police. Tiffany is back in the kitchen, bustling away at something or other. Her ponytail bobs in time to the tearing of kale for a salad. I reach for a bottle of Shiraz and hold it up toward her. She nods. We're at the breakfast nook within a few minutes, wine glasses in hand.

"What's wrong?"

"There is something nagging at me," I admit. I'm surprised. One, that my discomfort might show that obviously, and two, that, as always, Tiffany is perceptive enough to notice. She will make an excellent First Lady.

Now Tiffany is surprised. Openly. She is used to a husband who doesn't share; this is as second nature to her as breathing.

I can sense her eagerness. We've become the couple who shares. God, she'll probably want to cuddle later tonight.

"A detective came by to see me today. He thinks Norm was murdered."

"Oh, my God. Is Faye okay?"

Faye. Dammit. I didn't think to reach out to the family after Lin Raynes left. I ignore the question. "One thing the detective asked about was security. It appears Norm turned off the security system before he died, and when he did, there were seven people signed into the building."

Tiffany waits for me to continue. Honestly, I am not quite sure how to proceed. "But when I arrived, there were eight cars in the lot."

She doesn't miss a beat and doesn't ask how the hell I know that. Tiffany leans in. "What do you think that means?"

"I think it means there was someone else in the building. Probably the murderer."

And there it is. The thing that's been bugging me. The thing unspoken. The thing that could be my undoing.

Chapter 4

Tiffany is in seventh heaven. Her husband of five years has, at long last, confided something of real substance to her. They have connected on a deeper level. He loves her. At least, so goes her mind's fairy tale.

I can see Tiffany's wheels spinning. See the smile she tries so hard to hide; after all, this is a tragic incident we're discussing. But despite the different observations we bring to the conversation, I trust Tiffany's judgment in situations like this. It's about more than empathy. It's political savvy.

We're 37. I've spent perhaps the last 15 years planning a path to the presidency of the United States. I've dipped my toes in political waters and become familiar with its processes and the fine art of protectionism. Tiffany is up to her neck in those waters. It's all she has ever known. Her father, Senator John Williams, has been a pillar of the upper house since Moses ascended Mount Sinai. She has diplomatic acumen in her DNA.

For most people, the first question they'd ask after being told their husband might have seen a killer's car would be, *Are you sure*?

Tiffany either has the wisdom not to ask or the confidence there is no need. If I said there were eight cars in the lot, there were eight cars. I might not know how to interpret a glance between two people, but I can count to eight. I'm an observer of human life and the landscapes of those lives. That's in my DNA.

"Why are you reluctant to tell the detective?"

And with one question, my wife has nailed my dilemma. Tell Raynes, and I open myself up to scrutiny and potential blame. Tell Raynes, and the fact that Norm's death is not a suicide becomes real. Tell Raynes, and my cannabis company will feel the weight of every regulator this country has, and it has a lot.

"I'm worried he'll think I killed Norm. I'm worried this will harm the company," I finally reply.

"What are you worried about?" Tiffany looks me straight in the eye. It's not guesswork on her part.

My wife has posed the question I ultimately need to answer myself. In my hesitation, however, she answers for me.

"This will thrust you into uncharted waters, wrest control from you, and not be a comfortable experience for you." My 5'7", blonde-haired, blue-eyed, and very savvy wife does not turn away. "This is not about you. Tell the detective."

I must remember that line if Raynes asks me why I'm sharing this information because this is about helping Norm and his family.

Tiffany, as usual, is right.

* * *

The plan is to finish our wine, enjoy a delicious meatless lasagna (an oxymoron, I know), then call Raynes. We're sipping our first glass of Alto Estate when the doorbell rings. Guess who? And there go my plans.

"Sorry to interrupt," Raynes says, "but I'm hoping I might get a minute or two of your time."

"Come in," says Tiffany, who has floated up behind me unheard. So much for my powers of observation. "You must be the detective." Tiffany gently nudges me out of the way and ushers Raynes into the house. I assume we'd head for the living room, but Tiffany keeps walking toward the kitchen. Dammit. That means we will treat this man like a friend, not a guest. I know my wife.

"Lin Raynes." The detective holds out his hand and smiles. And another woman bites the dust.

"Would you like a glass of wine?" I ask in my role as the third wheel.

"We have beer." Tiffany returns his smile. "I have a Garrison Hoppy Buoy."

I have no idea what the fuck that means or what my wife keeps hidden in the inner workings of our refrigerator. She emerges from behind the fridge door, holding a brown glass bottle. Raynes nods his approval.

My wife melts a little more.

"Your wife has good taste in craft beer," he says by way of explanation, looking at me as if he knows I'm at a loss to explain what is happening in my own kitchen. "I probably shouldn't," he says, glancing now at Tiffany. "Duty and all that. But it is after my shift."

"Bottle or glass?"

"Bottle is fine." Of course, it is. This is Nova Scotia.

We settle around the breakfast nook. "Sorry to take you away from your dinner," Raynes says. Tiffany assures him it needs at least another 30 minutes. She gives me a sidelong steely gaze.

"Actually, I was hoping to speak with you," I say, perhaps a little too quickly.

Raynes does the thing with his left eyebrow.

"Why don't you two head to the den," Tiffany says. "I won't be in your way, and you won't be in mine."

I don't know what my wife is up to, but I know enough not to question her methods. Raynes and I take our drinks to the den. It's the messiest room in the house. Tiffany would tell you it's the most comfortable.

A small sectional sofa with throw pillows thrown everywhere takes up one wall. A black and glass desk with a black leather chair fills the opposite. This is the room where I work comfortably on Sundays and where Tiffany stretches out to read the latest mystery from Louise Penny or anything by Delia Owens. I don't know where Raynes fits, but the sofa seems to be the only viable option.

Raynes moves a few pillows out of the way and sits down like any typical Tuesday evening. "What's up?"

"Do you remember the list of names my IT manager gave us yesterday?" Raynes nods.

"There were seven names on the list. Names of people signed in before Norm turned off the security system."

Raynes patiently waits for me to continue. His attitude is laissez-faire, but I feel he is on high alert. "I don't know if it means anything, but when I arrived at 6:46, there were eight cars in the parking lot."

Raynes peers at me. He doesn't ask how I know, doesn't question my addition. Perhaps he believes that anyone who knows they arrived to work at 6:46 a.m. on a specific day is, by default, a car counter. "Do you know what car was out of place?"

Great freakin' question. While I didn't ask myself that specifically, I have been trying, unsuccessfully, to picture the cars in the lot that morning. I can remember a few, but I don't know who drives what in my company, so this is not something I pay particular attention to. "Sorry. I don't."

"So, someone else may have been in the building." It's unclear if Raynes is talking to himself or me.

"It looks that way." I answer in case he did want my input.

"This could be important. Do you have cameras in the parking lot?"

"You might catch the first row from the camera over the security login. But that will not help you much as employee cars get parked further back. We usually leave the front row for visitors and delivery."

"Can you get me a list of the cars driven by the seven people we know signed in early that morning?"

"I can try, but can't you do that on your end?"

"As a police officer, I can't access motor vehicle registration information without a good reason. And by good, I mean legal. If any of the seven on the early morning employee list were suspects, I would have free rein. However, simply being present in the building where you work when a crime is committed does not constitute probable cause."

So, the baton passes to me. "I'll have to check with Susan Warrington and Michael Graves, our in-house legal counsel. This might be a privacy issue." Canada is big on privacy. Revealing information without permission or even asking for certain types of information can land you in deep trouble, which I definitely want to avoid.

"I appreciate you trying." Raynes leans forward, and I figure I'm about to find out the reason for his visit.

Before he can say anything, Tiffany appears. "Dinner's ready," she says. "You're staying," she adds, looking at Raynes and making the definitive statement sound like an invitation. Her ponytail, I swear, bounced.

"Thank you. I'd enjoy a homecooked meal."

He smiles at me. I do not melt. Goddammit, now the man is going to eat a meal with us. I turn to him, lean in, and whisper, "It's plant based."

Now it's my turn to smile.

* * *

Dinner goes much better than I expect. Not only is Tiffany great with small talk, but Raynes is as well. I contribute when the topic seems safe, which turns out to be all of them, and I know my insight and comments will be taken as I intend them. However, one thing is missing from the meal: why is Lin Raynes in my home in the first place?

That tidbit remains until the last mouthful of dessert, a vegan apple crisp that surely comes second only to particle board. I reach for my exquisite organic Ethiopian yirgacheffe coffee when Raynes leans in. I brace.

"Not to cut this delightful dinner short, but I have a favour to ask." I relax a tinchlet, as the Nova Scotians say to describe something very small. "Faye Bedwell has agreed to talk to me this evening about her son being bullied. Riel, she'd like you to be there."

The use of my first name takes me aback, but not nearly as much as the request itself. I barely know this woman.

Raynes adroitly answers my unasked questions. "I think she would feel more comfortable if someone she knew was present, and she said you have been there for the family since her husband died."

I attempt not to gape. I look at Tiffany, who stares at her coffee cup. Ahh, so my wife has been reaching out. God bless her. I nod my acceptance. "Anything I can do."

"I suggest we get going," says Raynes. "I told Mrs. Bedwell we'd be there by 8:30."

Of course, he did.

* * *

Faye is waiting for us and much better than the last time I saw her. Her hair is combed, and she has mascara on her eyes. She's wearing black straight-leg pants that seem uncomfortable. A fuchsia cardigan adds a splash of color.

Tea is on the stove, a traditional Nova Scotia drink for family and friends who drop by, and in troubled times, a pot is always ready. It's Morse's, a local blend that has been around since 1879 when master brewer John. E. Morse opened up an import business on the Halifax waterfront.

Even though it comes from a bag, I enjoy the tea, and Tiffany has sent us armed with real Nanaimo bars (store-bought and not vegan). The evening resembles a social visit. I think Faye is in for a bit of a shock.

Again, I am wrong. Raynes had briefed Faye about the reason for our visit. I wish he had been as thorough with me. Not my week.

The detective dives right in. This time no smiles. "I'm sorry we have to do this, but we want to cross every *I* and dot every *T*."

Before he continues, Faye interjects. "You think Norm was murdered."

I'm glad I came. So happy, in fact, I almost grin. I ponder how wonder-boy will handle this. It turns out straightforward and terse.

Raynes looks directly at Faye and says only one word. "Yes."

It seems to satisfy her. A smile hovers at the corners of her mouth as a small rivulet of tears makes its way toward her chin. "My apologies. This is not something to celebrate, but what it means is Norm didn't want to leave us. He didn't plan to leave his family behind and broken."

It was almost poetic, and the reality of the words hit home. I understand what Faye is feeling. An emotion I am all too familiar with, relief. I reach over and pat her hand. I have no idea why I did that or where the gesture came from, probably Tiffany. Faye's expression tells me I did the right thing.

Raynes, however, can't hide his bewilderment. He is moving on to the reason for our visit, inquiring about the bullying. It turns out to be an unpleasant but not unanticipated tale. Bran, like his father, is short and round, a perfect patsy for the playground. He also does well in school and enjoys spending time with his parents. It's like he has a giant bullseye imprinted on his chest.

The main culprit, at least the one that landed everyone in the principal's office, is a kid named Simon Baillie. He's not short, not overweight, and not fond of his parents. In addition to the usual school ground confrontations, Simon launched an online campaign of relentless and hurtful ridicule. Once Bran broke down and told his parents about the abuse, a timeline unfolded that took many painful months. Faye and Norm approached the school. I already know from Susan Warrington that the outreach was unsuccessful, despite laws in place to clamp down on bullying and cyberbullying and mandating respectful relationships in schools.

Raynes knows this, too. "I understand that did not work."

"Baillie's parents are bullies themselves." Faye bristles. "There is no way they would admit their precious child did anything wrong. That might mean their behavior or their parenting was inappropriate. They might bear some of the blame. So, we sued them all. Sons of bitches." And Mama Bear comes out in full force.

I have seen this before with my parents. I never got bullied, but I was content to play alone in my younger years and remain outside the inner circle. My mother, Elena, was a constant thorn in my teachers' and principal's sides. And mine. She wanted her son to have friends and to be popular. Smart woman.

At present, we learn the case is in discovery. Faye's lawyer, a well-known and aggressive man who likes winning above all else according to his ads, has asked for all texts, emails, social media, and call logs. Raynes asks if he can see these. Faye agrees if her lawyer agrees.

We're ready to leave. Raynes thanks Faye and says he is sorry her family has to go through all this now.

She looks Raynes straight in the eye. "Tell the Baillies we're not backing down. No matter what." Then she turns to me and throws her arms around me. "Thank you."

"Any time," I say, stunned.

* * *

Tiffany is waiting up for me. A French press with Café Don Pablo decaf from Honduras is on the counter. I can't resist, which Tiffany knows well. There are also real cookies with gluten and dairy from a local bakery. The night is turning out much better than I anticipated.

"It went well," I say before my wife can ask. I'm already reaching for my second cookie. "Faye is having a rough time, but I suspect you know that." It's not a rebuke, just a fact.

"I've been calling to see how she and Bran are coping. We had coffee earlier this week."

"Thank you. I would not have thought of that."

"You're busy." Tiffany places her hand on mine. We both know she's lying. Being busy has nothing to do with why I didn't think to stay in touch with the Bedwells.

I recap the evening for her in some detail. I'm good with details, and my wife seems satisfied.

"Raynes likes you," she says out of left field.

"What are you talking about?" I am genuinely confused.

"It's not rocket science. Raynes wants to be friends." Tiffany doesn't wait for my counterargument. "What happens now?"

"It's out of my hands. Raynes takes over from here."

I couldn't have been more wrong. Again.

* * *

Susan Warrington is not as accepting of my car count as Lin Raynes. First thing on Wednesday morning, after my evening with the HPD detective, I call her into my office. She arrives with her Spidey senses tingling. I miss the signals until I ask if requesting plate numbers from employees is legal. It is like a chill wind blew down from the North Pole.

"What do you need that information for?" Susan asks. It is more of a challenge.

I explain to our protector of privacy laws that seven people signed into the building the day Norm died, but eight cars were in the lot. If we could identify the seven cars and their owners, it might help us with identifying the eighth vehicle.

"How do you know there were eight cars in the lot?" Susan asks. It's a challenge. "Did you count them?"

I did, but I'm not about to admit this to my director of HR. Lin Raynes is rapidly

69

rising up the ladder of "people I like." However, Susan's instantaneous response to my car-counting habit does raise the question why Raynes didn't ask me about my penchant for numbers. And now, for the first time, I have to answer the question. It's one I have anticipated in some form or another over the years. It's even one I have been asked in different and less murderous situations. I'm ready with an answer.

"I always check the lot for security purposes. At that hour of the morning, I like to see who's in the building."

"But you don't know who's in the building," Susan counters. The challenge is back. "All you know is how many people are in the building and not even that. If people carpooled, there could be a lot more people inside than cars outside."

I underestimate my 5' 4" HR director. I learned years ago, thanks in large part to my father-in-law, that when faced with a difficult or uncomfortable question, ignore it. Apparently, I have also created a culture where underlings feel comfortable openly confronting the CEO. I'll have to put a stop to that.

That's exactly what I do. "Is it possible to get car licenses, models, and makes from the employees signed in the morning Norm died?"

"I don't know." Susan appears to be debating the merits of the request.

"Should we bring legal in?"

"It wouldn't hurt. If the request isn't legal, the issue stops there. If it is, we'll have to grapple with the ethics of the request."

Before I can stop myself, I blurt out, "What ethics?"

"People need to feel safe where they work." Susan is talking as if to a six-year-old. Clearly, the company needs a culture shift. The image of a bug being squashed flashes across my eyes.

"I don't think asking employees to assist in the murder investigation of a valued colleague is stepping outside ethical lines." There is an edge in my voice. I'm assuming Warrington is astute enough to hear it.

Susan, mirroring my approach to difficult questions, switches gears. "Let's ask Michael for a legal opinion."

Michael Graves enters my office in two minutes, taking in Susan's presence as he strides confidently through the door. This is lawyering 101. Never let 'em see you sweat. "How can I help?"

I describe the information we're seeking and why. I don't tell him I counted the cars; I simply say there were eight cars in the lot and seven carded employees. Michael takes a minute. It's an uncomfortable minute. It's like he's going to break a tie and declare a winner. I sense he knows that and knows that Susan and I are on opposing sides.

"I'll have to confirm with a few pieces of legislation," Michael says, defaulting to lawyering 202, "but off the top, I don't see any legal barrier to requesting the information. Compelling the information may be a different matter.

"Of course," he continues, "anyone who doesn't comply is likely to come under suspicion. People will know that."

He takes a breath. "I should also declare a conflict. In all likelihood, one of the eight cars is mine. I was in the building that morning."

That's right. Michael let the cops inside. I point out that it's not the seven employee vehicles we're most interested in, it's the eighth. This request of employees is a process of elimination.

"Let me get back to you," Michael says.

We'll have our answer by noon.

* * *

I call Raynes to update our progress. I assure him Michael Graves is both very thorough and very competent. "We'll know soon enough whether we can proceed, but at first blush, it appears positive."

"Would you mind if I spoke to the group of employees about the request?" Raynes asks.

I can't think of an objection off the top of my head. Instead, I ask, "Why?"

"A couple of reasons. First, this can put you and your company in a bad light if there is pushback. Second, if the request comes from the police, it is an official ask out of your hands."

"I appreciate that." I'm sure the grin is evident in my voice, although I would not have pegged Lin Raynes as a man who goes out of his way to help companies embroiled in a murder investigation. "Something tells me that is not the main reason, though."

Raynes laughs. "Not even close. If I can see the responses to the ask, I can get a sense of who's uncomfortable or who's nonchalant. I can see if we should take a closer look at anyone."

And there it is. The ethical line Susan warned we might not want to cross. "Will that be a problem?" Raynes senses my hesitancy.

"I want employees to feel safe at work." I quote my HR director.

"Did Norm Bedwell feel safe?"

* * *

We have the legal green light to proceed with the parking lot request. Nothing in the various pieces of privacy legislation, federal or provincial, restricts asking employees to volunteer personal information. Compelling them to comply is another can of worms, and fortunately, one we do not have to open.

Susan, Michael, and I are back in my office discussing the process. None of us are getting any cannabis-related work done today. I'm not overly concerned. Our profit margin will be just fine, even if we don't work for a week or more. In 2020, the recreational cannabis market here hit $4.17 billion, triple the previous year, which also happened to be the first full year marijuana was legal in Canada.

I share Raynes's request to be included in the official ask with my two directors. To my amazement, Susan thinks it's a great idea. "Then it is a police issue. We can assure employees we have checked privacy legislation, and the request does not violate any laws."

Michael is also on board. It's decided to offer a modicum of protection to our people, and no one will be expected to step up at the meeting and volunteer their information. They can email the details to Susan. Or not.

We check work schedules, and everyone is in the building. Susan suggests we do this as quickly as possible, so people don't have time to worry about what's up or what type of trouble they might be in. I call Raynes while Michael and Susan reach out to supervisors. Everyone is on board.

An hour later, we're in the conference room in the admin building. Susan thinks this would be less intimidating than the boardroom. The room is arranged with small tables. There's coffee and Tim Hortons doughnuts, but no podium, PPT screen, or printed agenda. I smile my appreciation at Susan. "Marcia," she mouths slowly and silently. Of course. Somehow, the all-sensing individual who is my executive assistant attended to the details I didn't think of for this meeting. A meeting I didn't even know Marcia was aware of it.

Raynes, dressed in light brown khakis and a white long-sleeved t-shirt, looks like he has come to a weekly poker game with friends. His clothing is deliberate, I'm sure. I make a mental note to better align attire with purpose.

Both Raynes and Susan suggest that I open the discussion, so I welcome everyone and explain the police have a request in their ongoing investigation into the death of our colleague Norm Bedwell. I tell them we've reviewed the legislation, and the request is legal but not compulsory. Then I quickly hand the reins to Raynes. (First time I thought of using that alliteration.)

Raynes takes over and pulls no punches. "We need your help. As your CEO says, you're not obligated to assist us, but I'm hoping you will. It could help us solve Mr. Bedwell's murder."

Everyone gasps, including me. This is the first time the word has been openly used, and it's like a slap in the face. Even if, like me, you were aware of the situation or surmised it, now you know the truth.

"That's right," Raynes continues. His use of the word "murder" is deliberate, and he keeps the shock value to his advantage. "Someone murdered Mr. Bedwell. It's my job to find out who. And you can help."

He quickly explains that we're looking for the make, model, and license plate number of the car the employees drove and parked in the parking lot on the day Norm died. He doesn't mention the eighth car. He does make it clear the police do not suspect anyone in this room of murder. The inquiry is simply routine police work to confirm who was in the building, what cars were in the lot, and other details about the scene. Raynes takes a moment to look at the assembled group. He doesn't smile.

Susan quickly steps in. She reiterates that this information is voluntary and that no one is expected to provide it now. It can be emailed to her if anyone wants to do so. She asks if there are any questions.

A young man at a table to my left raises his hand uncertainly. I don't know him. I assume he must work in production. "Are we safe?" he asks. "I have two young kids."

Christ. I did not see this coming. I should have. Dammit, legal and HR should have seen it coming. Raynes should have seen it coming. The cannabis industry is new in Canada. Indeed, the country is breaking new ground internationally in this sector. There are a lot of naysayers – nasty, incensed naysayers who are predicting the end of the world because people can legally smoke weed. Many of them threaten violence to property. And people.

I am angry at my misstep and that of my colleagues, but anger does not mix well with psychopathy. I push it down. There is a compartment for this.

While I am not prepared for this question, I'm out of my chair and in front of the room in seconds. "I want to assure everyone that you are safe and encourage you to share this with your coworkers. Your safety is our number one priority. We are doing everything we can to protect you and will continue to do everything possible."

Susan and Raynes are standing beside me now. Susan tells everyone there have been no reported problems. Raynes goes a step further. "Between us," he says, knowing this will make its way through the building within minutes of the meeting ending, "murders are generally a crime motivated for personal reasons by someone who knows the victim well or for whom the victim represents an obstacle. We have no indication at all that this crime was anything other than that. As far as we have found in our investigation, you are all safe as Riel said."

I appreciate the support. I'm a bit taken aback by the use of my first name in this more formal context, but I realize it's a smart move. It makes it sound like the police have been keeping us in the loop, so we can protect employees if necessary. And it makes us sound like we are all one family, not workers and a CEO.

We end on that note. As employees are filing out the door, they come up to shake my hand. I work not to gape. There is nothing wrong with the culture in this company.

* * *

Something had occurred to me as the meeting got under way. I glance around for Raynes as I shake the last hand. It's the young man.

"Thank you," he says. "I really like working here. Now I know why." The young man doesn't wait for my response. He turns and heads out the door.

I turn to see if Raynes has left, and somehow he is standing in front of me. "I thought we could take a minute to chat." I nod in the direction of the door.

Raynes nods back. "Let's get out of here. There's a Starbucks across the street."

I don't mind Starbucks. It has some acceptable coffee, although they brew the bejesus out of it. Good grief, now I'm sounding like a Nova Scotian. I order a sundried Ethiopia Sidamo. It has a deep roasted flavour with an aroma of chocolate and cherry, and it's a limited edition. I'll enjoy it while I can. Unlike the conversation about to follow.

Raynes does not point to a random coffee urn but instead orders a pumpkin-spiced latte. He registers my expression. "Reminds me of Thanksgiving with my mother. She's in Ontario with my brother for the holiday."

His obvious fondness for his mother reminds me that I haven't called my parents in a while. I make a mental note to do that tonight. Once we're seated in a quiet corner of the coffee shop, because the lunch crowd has not yet landed, I dive in and say, "There is something I didn't think to mention, but the info session reminded me."

Raynes raises his left eyebrow.

I'm unsure if this gesture is the equivalent of a thumb's up or mild rebuke. I continue. "We get a lot of nasty mail. Cannabis is new to Canada, and some think it's the devil in disguise."

"I may be one of those," says Raynes with a grin. "I worked narcotics for two years and saw things I never want to see again." He takes a breath. "How bad is the vitriol?"

"I don't know," I answer frankly. "Aside from emails that come to individual mailboxes, which are few, most hateful comments and threats are made on social media. We've had a few actual letters. Neela Khoury, our IT manager, monitors the online comments. Susan Warrington in HR gets everything else. Anything that stands out to either of them gets sent to legal."

"Has anything stood out?"

"There were three threats against the company directly, but that was a while ago. I'll have Michael dig out everything he thinks may be helpful."

"Now it's my turn," Raynes says. "I have another favour to ask."

I stiffen. Lin Raynes's favours inevitably take me outside my comfort zone.

"I have an interview with the Baillies this afternoon. I was hoping you could join me."

I don't even try to mask my confusion. "How could I possibly help?" Apparently, I'm more honest about my feelings than I realized.

Raynes laughs. "I don't need you to ask questions or vet any information. But I need a Norm Bedwell barometer."

"If I knew what that was, I might be better able to determine if I could help." Yet more honesty.

Raynes responds with one of his smiles. "Solving a murder is often more about understanding the victim than unearthing evidence. I don't know what would have set Bedwell off, pushed him to antagonize others, or put him in the crosshairs of a killer. You can help me with that."

Before I can interject, Raynes continues. "Bullying is a hot-button issue. One that would have any parent seeing red. I need to understand how Bedwell was likely to react – not what he did, but what he may have been feeling."

I feel like there is something I'm missing. "Wouldn't Norm's wife be a better barometer? Or his sister?"

"The wife is too close, and I wouldn't ask her to subject herself to a meeting with the parents of the kid hurting her son. The sister is back in Cape Breton, but even then, I would be hesitant to ask her for the same reasons."

"Susan Warrington knew Norm better than I did. What about her?" I realize that my questions may sound like excuses. Helping the police is something a good CEO and future president of the United States would do without question. "It's not that I don't want to help, but I may not be best person in this case."

"You'll be great," Raynes says. "You won't let emotion cloud your judgment."

Now, what the fuck does that mean?

Chapter 5

Susan Warrington is waiting in my office when Raynes and I get back. "I have the information on the automobiles for you," she says without any preamble. Both Raynes and I are taken aback.

"What do you mean?" I ask sub-intelligently.

"I have the make, model, and colour for the seven employee-owned vehicles in the parking lot when you arrived that morning." Susan is obviously and obscurely referencing the day Norm Bedwell died. She sounds huffy like somehow this whole process has offended her.

"Thank you," Raynes says. "You've been so helpful."

The chill leaves Susan. It's like Raynes has a magic wand. The HR director looks at me, and some of the chill returns. "You should be proud of these people. And you should tell them that."

Marcia appears in the doorway. "I'll draft something for you," she says quietly. "I'm assuming these will be individual emails."

I nod but have no idea what is going on.

Marcia glances at me. "Would you like me to ask Michael to step in?" I'm glad this woman is on my side.

"Would you like me to stay?" Susan asks, sensing something is up.

Both Raynes and I nod. "Thank you." I'm a fast learner.

Michael arrives around the same time Marcia returns with coffee and biscotti. "Thought you might all need a little something."

The little something turns out to be a honey-processed caturra from Costa Rica. I find myself mellowing with the first sip, then I look at Raynes. There is no nod, but somehow, he understands I have turned the meeting over to him. After all, he is the detective. I'm just trying to run a damn cannabis plant.

"We were thinking about hate mail," he says, diving in head first. Both Michael and Susan visibly relax. Whatever they thought we'd be talking about, hate mail is more comforting.

"What are you looking for?" Michael asks.

"I don't know," Raynes says. "You tell me. What should I be searching for?"

Michael and Susan shoot each other a glance, not conspiratorial but confused. I'm with them.

Raynes picks up on the uncertainty. "I understand cannabis is a hot-button issue," he says, quoting me. "I assume much of the anti-fan mail that comes your way is run of the mill. I'm looking for the stuff the mill didn't anticipate."

Now the look that passes between Susan and Michael is conspiratorial. I find myself sitting a little straighter. Raynes leans in.

"Anything we were concerned about, we passed on to the Halifax Police Department," Michael says offering up an unasked-for explanation or excuse.

"I have no doubt you've done everything by the book," says Raynes, leaning forward.

"You have to understand no one was ever threatened directly, and certainly Norm was never mentioned by name," Michael says, continuing to offer up his penance.

Susan has had enough. "There were three posts that, quite frankly, concerned us. They were from the same person, but we do not know who that person is. The police investigated. They got no further than we did. There was never a fourth post, so we assumed the person ran out of steam."

Neither Susan nor Michael looks at me or even in my direction, a hard feat to accomplish in an office with only four people. This information was never shared with me. I wonder why.

"I'll have Jennifer email the file." Susan starts texting her assistant. A few minutes later, we're staring at copies of the three posts, all of which appeared on Bible Belt, a popular fundamentalist site, all posted by someone called @frommylips. The content isn't pleasant, but perhaps because I've been steeling myself for what is about to come, the hate isn't as violent or ugly as I imagined. There are several references to rotting in hell and a clear indication that the writer is prepared to pave the way.

"This guy thinks you're doing the work of the devil, but I doubt that is anything new," says Raynes. "What made these stand out?"

"These were the only posts we read that seemed to threaten the safety of staff," Michael says. Sure enough, @frommylips writes that any heathens who cross the threshold of CCC will die a fiery, painful death. It is unclear, however, what specific heathens, if any, are being targeted.

"The fire and brimstone rhetoric could be a reference to hell," Raynes points out.

"Or it could be a forewarning of arson," says Susan with a hint of snark. "Either way, he was the only one to ever make a reference to personal safety, and we take the security of our employees very seriously."

I would like to see how this plays out; I honestly could not pick a winner between the two, but again, I'm trying to run a company. "Is there any way to find out who sent these?" I ask Raynes, hoping to melt the ice and move the floes along.

"I should know by the end of the day," he says, "unless we're dealing with someone who is online savvy. I'm guessing that is not the case from the quality of these posts."

Raynes is already grabbing his jacket and making his exit. "Thank you, everyone. I'll be in touch." The latter, I'm surmising, was intended for me.

Susan and Michael start to follow suit.

"If you have a moment," I say. The ice is back.

* * *

At last, I have my office to myself. The paperwork has piled up, which is always uncomfortable for me. Control depends on organization. I don't like getting behind or derailed. I jump in, comfortable in this role, comfortable knowing what to do next. I tackle the email first, then start returning calls.

I'm in my comfort zone for about two hours before Raynes calls. The meeting with the Baillies is set for 5:30. "It's not ideal," says Raynes. "Hungry parents, cranky kid. But they wanted to meet as soon as possible."

We agree Raynes will pick me up at the office at 5 p.m. Traffic in Halifax is light, even when locals think it's bumper to bumper. In 30 minutes, maybe 40, you can get from downtown to the outskirts of the city – and that's in five o'clock traffic. The Baillies live in Elmsdale, on Hescott Street. We can be there in a few minutes from my office on the outskirts of town, near the Halifax Stanfield International Airport, which is about a half hour from the city when it isn't rush hour. Tiffany and I live in Grand Lake, about 15 minutes from the office heading to the city, so it makes sense to meet at CCC.

I call Tiffany to let her know dinner will be delayed.

"I'm glad you're helping Lin." She's as pleased as punch. "That's very nice of you."

I notice Tiffany is on a first-name basis with the detective now. She's aware of what Raynes has asked of me and why. She seems to think this makes perfect sense. I'm not buying it, but I don't see that I have any option other than to help. However, what I understand that Tiffany doesn't is that my connection with Raynes will end when he solves Norm Bedwell's murder. I'm convinced he's right; Norm likely did not kill himself. And surprisingly, there is a growing list of suspects. I'll do what Raynes asks, but this is not about a budding bromance. It's about meeting expectations and getting the hell back to my comfort zone.

* * *

I'm in my office putting a few files into my briefcase when Raynes strolls in.

He's prompt. Naturally. "All set?"

"Anything you want me to bring or do?" I reach for my coat.

"There's no game plan to this type of interview. It will depend on the response we get from the Baillies."

"Something tells me it won't be pleasant."

"Something tells me you're right."

Hescott Street is part of an established residential area in Elmsdale. It resembles a country lane in many ways. Houses are older and large, although more modern homes are being built on the available land. The Baillies live in a two-storey, beige-shingled home that has likely been in the family for decades.

Vanessa Baillie opens the door before we have a chance to knock. She is a thin woman with dark, well-styled hair. Her nails are manicured, clothes pressed, lips pursed. She reminds me of a mannequin.

Mother Baillie ushers us in without saying a word. Raynes smiles, but his charm is falling flat. It is unclear whether we are inviting disdain or causing distress, maybe both. We make our way to the living room. It appears like a hasty clean-up has been conducted. A small stack of magazines peeks out from a mound of burgundy pillows consuming a cream sofa. Video games form a ramshackle tumble on the bottom of a TV cabinet. Without a preamble or waiting for seating instructions, Raynes pulls a chair closer to the cherrywood coffee table and the sofa. I wonder if this is calculated. I sit a little further back in an over-stuffed armchair.

A man of medium height, medium build, and medium brown hair enters the room. I find it hard to believe this couple has raised a bully, and they didn't crumple like a stack of cards when told their son was one.

There is no offer of coffee or refreshments on the table, so much for Nova Scotia niceties. Raynes thanks the Baillies for meeting with us. Then he asks for a glass of water. Vanessa asks if I'd like one. I follow Raynes's lead.

While our water is being poured, Mr. Medium introduces himself. "I'm William. Simon's dad."

I can't believe someone named their kid Bill Baillie. Parents have no concept of what it's like for offspring to grow up with attributes ripe for ridicule. I realize Vanessa is back and icily asking how they can help. She's undoubtedly the alpha in the family. And now Simon's nasty behaviour begins to make some sense.

"We wanted to learn a little more about the situation with the Bedwells," Raynes says, his neutral tone and facial expression friendly and bland. William relaxes, but Vanessa isn't buying the nice-guy routine.

"The situation is they accused our son of something he absolutely did not do." Vanessa's tone is angry; her chin lifted in defiance.

I'd squash her like a bug, then wonder what Raynes would do.

He plays the dumb cop. "What did they accuse Simon of doing?"

William is about to explain. Vanessa doesn't give him a chance. "You damn well know what they accused him of. We're not stupid."

Raynes waits a few seconds and then stares directly at Vanessa. His tone matches hers, icicle for icicle. "A man is dead – a man who had an issue with you and your family. You can answer our questions here or down at the station. The choice is yours."

So, there he is, the man who made detective. Mr. Nice Guy has left the building.

William doesn't wait for Vanessa to dig them in any deeper. "We'll answer your questions."

I'm impressed with the response. It's not obsequious, nor is it defiant.

Raynes dismisses Vanessa and turns to William. He adjusts his position on the chair, so his back is slightly toward the wife. "I'd like to hear your side."

"Simon is a good kid. He does well in school and has lots of friends. One day we get a call from the principal's office saying Simon is accused of bullying another student, and we're called in for a meeting." William peers at the floor. "It didn't go well."

"What happened?" Raynes asks.

Vanessa opens her mouth. William cuts her off. Smart man. "They were accusatory. We were defensive. They had stuff they said Simon posted, but no proof."

"Did you speak to Norm Bedwell after that meeting?" Raynes asks.

William turns to his view of the floor again. He hesitates. "No. I didn't."

I take this at face value, but Raynes understands the loophole William has used. He turns to Vanessa. "Did you speak with Norm Bedwell after this meeting?"

The bravado is gone. She looks at Raynes. "Yes."

Raynes looks back. "I'll need more."

"The Bedwells are nasty people." Vanessa is focused straight ahead. I'm unsure at what. Maybe she is reliving the incident in her mind. "After that awful meeting, I couldn't stop thinking about what those horrible people were doing to my son. I didn't sleep. I went to work and couldn't concentrate, so I called Bedwell at that drug place where he works."

"What happened?" Raynes asks.

"He told me my son was a bully. I told him that was simply not true, and we left it at that. We agreed to let the lawyers settle things." Vanessa looks directly at Raynes once more. Her lips start to curl up; she suppresses a grin. I have no idea what she is smiling about, but I'm beginning to understand the complexity of Raynes's job.

I will never know why I did what I did next, and convinced it was not prudent. I lean in, attempt to appear nonchalant, and ask Vanessa, "Did you say you called Bedwell on his work line?"

"Yes." Her gaze shifts to me. I see relief. That was a misstep. I glance back at Vanessa, at William, and then at Raynes. "That may be helpful. CCC's network allows calls on all extensions and direct lines to record automatically. That call is likely available if Norm did not delete his cache, and most of us don't."

Now, it's Raynes who's suppressing a grin. William has gone white; Vanessa is furious. "You have no right to record a private call," She's almost shouting. "My lawyer will destroy you."

I hate to admit it, but I'm enjoying this. "Under federal law, as long as one person knows a conversation is being recorded, it is perfectly legal to record that conversation. Norm knew calls were recorded; all CCC employees know this. It's in their employment contracts, and frankly, it's there to protect them."

I have them stymied now and go for the finale. "In addition, the answering system software tells all callers conversations are recorded for quality assurance." I don't know what the hell that means, but I've heard it often enough.

William is now slumped on the sofa. Any fight he had is gone out of him. "I don't know what was said specifically on that call, but I know Vanessa said she'd make him pay. She said no one accuses her son of being a bully and gets away with it."

"So, what," hisses Vanessa, any pretense of nicety gone. "Free speech."

"You may want to read the laws in this country and this province more carefully," says Raynes. "Threats against a person constitute assault under the *Criminal Code*."

"What do you want?" Vanessa snaps. "We didn't kill the man, but I'm glad he's dead. He got what he deserved."

William stares at his wife. He's aghast.

I give the marriage another six months at most.

He turns to Raynes. "When did Mr. Bedwell die?"

"Wednesday, October 14th, in the early morning hours."

"Vanessa was home in bed with me," William says. "I'm a light sleeper. I would know if she left the bedroom."

He anticipates Raynes's next question. "I know a husband's word doesn't count for much, but you can check the GPS on her car and mine. Every trip will be accounted for. Neither of us drove to the cannabis company."

Vanessa's expression doesn't change. My guess: William is telling the truth. "Our techs will be by first thing in the morning," Raynes says. "Can you let me know what you both drive?"

"I have a 2018 Honda Civic, and Vanessa has a 2016 Volvo XC90," William says.

"Colours?" Raynes asks to everyone's confusion.

"My car is white, and Vanessa's is silver," Williams says. Raynes shoots me a glance. I have no idea why. Then it occurs to me – the mystery car in the parking lot. But despite Raynes's hopefulness, I am no further ahead at remembering the description of that vehicle.

"Are you through?" Vanessa asks. The snark is back.

"Just one more thing," Raynes says. I couldn't imagine what more he wanted. Nor could the Baillies. We were both about to be given a jolt.

* * *

Raynes asks if he can speak with Simon. William says, "Yes." Vanessa asks, "Why?"

Raynes says he'd like to help clear up the issue between the two families and end the trauma for everyone, if possible. Avoid the cost of lawyers and the stress of court. Pretty hard after that for either parent to refuse the request.

On Simon's entry into the living room, he quickly gives Raynes and me the once-over and dismisses us. It may be his stature, his mother's genetics, or he doesn't realize an HPD detective is in the house, but this kid knows no fear. So, mom and dad didn't tell him the police would be dropping by.

Simon Baillie is a big boy, about 100 pounds and 5'4". I wonder what side of the family he gets that from. Some pediatrician somewhere will put him in the 98th percentile for boys his age. The kid is muscular; I'm guessing he plays football, maybe b-ball.

Simon turns to his parents. Their expressions must bother him because now he looks back at Detective Raynes. Simon turns to his mother. "What's up?"

Raynes answers. "I was hoping we could clear up the matter with the Bedwells." He extends his hand. "I'm Detective Lin Raynes with the Halifax Police Department."

At this point, Simon has two choices: swagger or deference. I'm guessing he'll pick door number one, and I'm right.

With a simple shrug, the 12-year-old bully dismisses Raynes's credentials and any threat implied by a police presence in his home. Vanessa doesn't hide her approval. William wisely has a less confident bluster, which seems the best approach with a man like Raynes. His instincts are spot on.

Raynes ignores the implied insult and smiles. "I'd like to hear it from you. What has happened between you and Bran Bedwell?"

"The kid's a pansy." I swear Simon sneered. "I didn't touch him."

"No one says you physically touched him," Raynes clarifies, "but I understand there have been some unsettling social media and digital posts."

"So?" The kid can sneer without disruption.

"That would be against the law," says Raynes, "if it's true, of course."

Simon sees an opening. "Bedwell's a liar. I never said nothing to him."

"Or about him?" Raynes leads the kid where he wants him to go.

I'm not sure where that is.

"Like I said, I didn't say nothing to him or about him." Simon continues to sneer. "He's a wuss."

Papers have appeared in Raynes's hand, like a magician unveiling a flock of doves from thin air. "Would you mind if we just went through the posts and documented that you didn't say these things?"

William is savvy enough to know something is afoot. His wife and his son are too cocky at this point to catch on. The protective father makes a move forward, perhaps to stop the discussion or redirect it. Vanessa puts out a hand and stops him.

That doesn't go unnoticed by Simon. Now he has Mama's approval.

Raynes goes through each text, Instagram post, email, and Facebook message. Simon denies them all, and some are outright offensive, even to me. It's unclear if Simon is calling into question Bran's sexual orientation, bravery, intelligence, or his right to live, but these posts would wither the strongest adult. I have no idea where a 12-year-old would get such language, opinions, or hate, but I'm guessing the answer may be sitting on the couch across from me.

The list of vicious posts is long, but Raynes goes through them quickly, which is easy since Simon denies he sent any of them. I wonder if that's the point. When Raynes gets to the last post, he locks eyes with Simon. "I just want to confirm – again – that you did not ever call Bran Bedwell…" he glances down at the sheaf in his hand as if seeking out specific phrases and then continues, "a flaming fag, a fucking fudgepacker, or a spineless swish?"

Simon is grinning openly now. "Nope. Never said any of that."

Raynes nods, looking a little puzzled. He stares directly at Simon. "You see, here's the problem, the messages all trace back to your phone, laptop, or IP address. That's going to be an issue in court."

"I don't think so." Simon has a smile cemented to his face.

I think I liked it better when he sneered.

Raynes smiles back just as broadly. And more confidently. "Aah, you're referring to the VPN."

The detective senses the adult confusion in the room. "A virtual private network is a special server that encrypts a user's connection to the internet and hides their IP address. Amateur hackers and cyberbullies think we can't trace the code back to them. They're wrong."

Now Vanessa sees the trap, but she's not quick enough to stop her son as he says, "So what? Even if I wrote the stuff, there's nothing you can do."

Mama bear is about to move in.

Raynes raises his right hand and stops her cold. "Very astute," he says to Simon, who's too smug to see what his parents see. "Let me get this straight," Raynes says with an open grin. "You wrote this? Wow."

Simon nods. "I wrote everything."

"Everything on the list I have?" Raynes sounds impressed.

"The guy's a fag," says Simon. "It's a disease, you know."

William, obviously mortified, can't stop himself at this point. "Simon, how could you? How could you do that to another kid? How could you think that?"

"It's a sin." Simon says this as if his newfound religion justifies his actions. It doesn't work with his father. What his mother thinks is less obvious, but a part of me believes she may be siding with dad.

Raynes shrugs off buddy mode and transforms back into an HPD detective. "Here's the problem, and it is a big one." Raynes looks at Vanessa, William, and Simon one at a time. "These messages constitute cyberbullying, a crime in Nova Scotia. Much more serious, however, is that some of them also constitute a hate crime. That is a federal offense. That will likely mean time in jail."

Everyone is a little stunned at this pronouncement, including me. Surely, we don't send 12-year-olds to jail in Canada. (I later learn we sent kids 12 to 17 years of age to a special jail called a youth detention facility). Part of me wants to applaud soundly punishing bullies like Simon Baillie, another part wonders how this would play out with liberal voters in the 19th senate district in the state of California.

Simon isn't buckling under the threat of jail time. His confidence is remarkable. I'm about to learn it's not confidence. It's ignorance. "You can't touch me," he says confrontationally to the 6'4" cop in front of him. "Truth is a defence. Bedwell's a gay."

Raynes sighs. He gazes at the parents with dismay. "What your family knows about the law in this country could be contained on the head of a pin." Raynes turns back to Simon. "Truth is a defence against defamation. You are not accused of defamation. You are accused of bullying and hate crimes. And you have admitted your guilt."

"I take it back." Simon sounds slightly panicked, realizing he got played.

"You can't take it back," Raynes says.

"I'll say I never said any of this to you." Simon is a little like a raccoon trapped in a compost bin. All eyes and bristles.

"But you did say it, and you said it in front of witnesses," Raynes says.

"We'll deny it," Vanessa says.

The shocked expression is back on her husband's face. I'm sorry for the man, not empathetically, of course. More along the lines of the poor bastard can't get a break.

"You can deny it all you want." Raynes looks at me. "I have another witness."

Now I wonder if this is why I was invited. Just how clever and how wily is the detective?

"I also have the conversation recorded." Raynes points to his phone on the table.

"You can't do that," Vanessa says, grasping at straws. "You told us conversations with more than two people couldn't be taped without permission."

"Not what I said," says Raynes, "but it doesn't matter. The recording is my notes.

Police officers are expected to keep accurate notes when interviewing witnesses and suspects."

"But you didn't have our permission to check the origin of the messages," Vanessa says, grasping at straws.

"Didn't need it," says Raynes. "I came here to interview a family about a matter potentially connected to a murder I'm investigating. I'm obligated to review the evidence and investigate thoroughly."

The Baillie family finally acquiesces. The wind has gone out of whatever sails remained. "What do you want?" William asks, resigned.

"It's not up to me," says Raynes, sounding almost genial. I swear he may be bouncing slightly. "I'm not investigating the bullying charges. However, if Ms. Bedwell files a complaint, and I mean, who wouldn't, it will be evidence in the complaint, both criminal and civil. I'm obligated by law to turn this information over to our cyberbullying unit."

And there it is. Simon is screwed. Mom and dad can't win against Faye Bedwell in court, and their precious little browbeater could end up in juvie. I'd do a little dance if I cared about right and wrong.

"We'll have our lawyer call the Bedwells' lawyer tomorrow," says William. "Simon will also apologize to Bran online and in person, and to the principal." William turns to look directly at Raynes. It's clear he doesn't care what his wife or his son have to say. Again, if I cared…

"Our technicians will be over tomorrow morning to check out your cars," Raynes says. As he turns to leave, his back to the Baillies, he catches my eye and raises his left eyebrow.

Chapter 6

As if by mutual agreement, Raynes and I don't say a word to each other as we walk to the car. It's a glorious fall day, and the leaves – russet, auburn, crimson – wave from a grove of maple and oak trees. I should be enjoying the crisp fall air and the infusion of color in what has been an admittedly grey week. Instead, I reflect on what just happened and what it means for me, primarily, but also if Raynes's interview gets the police any closer to finding out who killed Norm Bedwell. I'd like that resolved so my life can go back to normal. Ahh, apparently, it is all about me.

Raynes is sauntering. I'm assuming he's unperturbed. That assumption is verified and refuted once we settle inside the car.

"Well, they're a piece of work." Raynes presumes I'll know what he means.

I do. "Did tonight help?"

"It did," says Raynes. "Vanessa and Simon are spiteful people. But frankly, they don't have the brains or the restraint to pull off Bedwell's murder. And William doesn't have it in him. "Can you believe someone named their kid Bill Baillie?" He turns to me with a grin.

I had no idea that thought would have occurred to anyone else. I must tell Tiffany the father's name. See if she gets the misnomer. "I didn't see the takedown of Simon Baillie coming." I'm unsure if the manoeuvre is something cops-to-be learn at the academy, something that comes with on-the-job experience, or something uniquely Lin Raynes.

The detective is quick to answer, "I don't like bullies. I particularly don't like people who are homophobic or who raise their children to be."

I don't know how to interpret that or if any interpretation is required. I don't like bullies either; it is stupid, unproductive behaviour. There is no nuance and no payoff. But I wonder if Raynes is telling me something more, perhaps that he's gay. It doesn't matter. The moment has passed. I'm unsure of what I would have done, even if time had allowed me to go further down this path.

"I also thought it might be nice to give Faye Bedwell a break. She has lost her husband. No need to pour more unpleasantness on her."

That would not have occurred to me.

"Will you follow up with her to see if the Baillies back off?" Raynes asks.

I'm caught off guard, and it shows.

"As a detective working a murder case, I can't stick my nose in issues outside my purview."

"Sure," I say quickly. "I've been reaching out to Faye fairly regularly."

Up goes Raynes's left eyebrow.

"Well, mostly Tiffany has been reaching out."

Raynes nods. That seems to make sense to him. "You helped me get Vanessa to own up to her actions. The recording information was critical."

Now this is a little awkward for me. I do like compliments, but I don't particularly appreciate taking credit for something that could potentially get me in hot water down the road.

Raynes senses my hesitation. "What's up?"

"I lied." I have no other option but the truth.

"Son of a bitch." Raynes tosses his head back and laughs out loud.

"Can that get you in any trouble?" What I want to know is if it can get me in trouble.

"You're a civilian. You provided information that was both unsolicited and unrehearsed. I didn't know you were making it up. I'm in the clear," Raynes says. "So are you. I noticed you never said all calls were automatically recorded or that Bedwell recorded his calls. You put out a reasonable hypothetical, and they panicked. That was smart thinking and careful wording."

"It was probably luck." I am lying and telling the truth at the same time. "I had no plans to do that. I just opened my mouth and talked. I was probably more surprised than the Baillies."

The laughter is back. "I did a little lying of my own," says Raynes.

I'm intrigued. Thinking back quickly over the evening, I can't find a time when I thought Raynes was anything but forthright.

"We don't have the kid's IP address linked to the messages. Now we don't need it. He's confessed."

"But you said you had traced the messages directly to Simon." I point this out needlessly.

"I did, and as a police officer, I am under no obligation to tell the truth when I'm conducting interviews, especially if there are suspects in the room."

"That's very deceitful and very clever."

"And very legal." The laugh is back.

I relax. "What was the thing about the colour of the cars?" I'm sure I know the answer to this, but I want to confirm. I also want to understand how much is expected of me.

"I thought it might help you. You saw eight cars in the lot the night Bedwell was killed. I was hoping this might trigger something."

"It doesn't quite work that way."
Turns out it does.

* * *

I realize Raynes is not heading to my office but driving toward my house. "Oh, I thought you knew. Tiffany invited me to dinner. She said she would drive you to the office in the morning."

Of course, she did. If I check my texts, one will be from her letting me know after the fact. "Glad you can join us," I say. To my surprise, I mean it. Raynes is sharp, and I'm learning skills from him that I'll use as a politician and a CEO.

Tiffany has wine open, cold beer in the fridge, and munchies on the table when we arrive. The menu choices have expanded. One bowl looks remarkably like Covered Bridge sea salt and pepper potato chips, my favorite. The dip does not appear to be hummus ground painstakingly by humans tethered to the land. I like it when the detective comes to dinner.

We head for the kitchen. It seems the place we gather with Raynes. Usually, it would be the living room. Tiffany appears nonchalant, which means something more important is on her mind than our meeting with the Baillies. That "something" would be to cement my "friendship" with Raynes. I know Tiffany's heart is in the right place, but friendships are not my forte.

"Everything go okay?" she asks.

"I could tell you," Raynes says, "but then I'd have to lock you away in a dark cell in a black-ops site. Easier just to wait until I leave, and Riel can tell you."

We all laugh. Ice broken, we move on to other issues, some light, some less so. Dinner flies by. I find myself taking fewer mental notes and starting to loosen up. I will get through this and come out stronger and smarter.

We're sipping coffee and eating some carob vegan thing Tiffany swears is a brownie. It's not. The coffee, however, is exquisite. A shade-grown Nicaraguan bean, and knowing Tiffany, it's 100 percent organic, chemical-free, fair trade, and non-GMO. Even Raynes is impressed, and he drinks beer.

Raynes and I are cleaning up, and Tiffany has left us to our own devices. She hopes we'll bond.

"What happens now?" I ask.

"We'll officially eliminate the Baillies, but I think we can take that as a foregone conclusion. So, I keep digging."

"What is there left to dig?" I wonder, then realize I've wondered out loud.

"That's the quintessential question in police work. What did I miss? What rock did I forget to peek under?"

"How do you answer those questions?"

"You go back to square one and go over everything again. You keep poking and prodding."

It's a technique that pays off, as I discover at 4:26 a.m.

* * *

I live in a world where people give a shit; they hug each other because they want to connect, and they cry when others hurt. I don't feel these things. But I have learned that to succeed in this world, to get what I want, I need to mirror the emotions second nature to most people and foreign to me. That makes me highly observant, even when I'm not consciously trying to take note of something.

I counted eight cars in the parking lot the day Norm Bedwell was murdered, an exercise in tallying, not an observation of makes, models, colours, and contrasts. When you know how many people are inside, you have a better sense of what you are walking into. The more people, the more disruption, and the more you need to be on alert.

I start reliving the morning in the parking lot around 2 a.m. when it becomes clear I'm not going to get a good night's sleep. At 2:48, I give in and go to the kitchen. I treat myself to a pot of Kona peaberry, medium roast. A cup of pure heaven but the moment is not about enjoyment; I dig out the list of cars Susan Warrington had assembled and walk through the parking lot a dozen times in my mind.

I park at the back end of the lot, on the left. As CEO, I'm entitled to a spot up front, an advantage in winter weather and early mornings. But I like the walk across the lot. In addition to counting cars, it gives me a buffer before I reach the front door. With a few mini-meditations and mantras, I'm better prepared for what lies ahead.

That day, I want to say that fateful day, I climb out of my car, a blue mica Lexus GS. No other vehicle is near mine. I close the door and reach for the lock. I hear the reassuring beep that the car is alarmed.

I raise my head, and the first car I see is at the other end of the lot from me. Small, white, two-door. I don't know cars, so I flip open my laptop and bring up an image for each of the seven on the list. I recognize the 2017 Nissan Micra as the small white two-door.

I continue on my mental journey across the lot walking toward the office with my briefcase. Two cars are ahead of me. One is a blackish SUV, the other a silver four-door. I cross the Kia Sorento and the Toyota Camry off my list.

I'm mentally midway to the front door with three cars ahead of me. One is Norm's white Honda Accord. One is red and easily knocked off the list. The other is a silver SUV, another Kia, a popular manufacturer.

I'm short two. I walk the path from my car to the front door again. And again. After about 12 trips across the lot, I remember reaching down to grab my briefcase after I locked the door. I looked back. Slate grey car. Electric. We've installed a charging station at the back of the parking lot, part of our efforts to reduce our carbon footprint. Now, I'm seven for seven. Where the hell is the eighth car?

Three cups of coffee and one vegan brown thing later, I decide retracing my steps is futile and focus on arriving at the front door.

I recall seeing that the security system wasn't set. I remember glancing around to see if someone had just turned it off or if something more sinister was hovering nearby. I scanned left, and then I scanned right. I can feel my anger.

And there it is. Midway in the parking lot a flash of something that resembles a giant carrot. I zero in on the color, and the whole thing comes into focus. A small orange truck is tucked out of the way, but once you've seen it, unmistakable. A vehicle that does not belong to anyone who signed into the CCC security system.

Now, it's almost 4:30 in the morning, and there's no going back to bed. I make breakfast, a cheese omelet with Balderson's cheddar from an actual cow and leave enough for Tiffany. She'll like the sentiment, even if she prefers something stemming from a plant.

I shower and dress. It's only 5:45. Too early to call Raynes, although he's likely an early riser, I say to myself. Or it may be me justifying what I'm about to do. At 5:50, I call Raynes.

He answers on the second ring. "You know it's not even 6 o'clock in the morning."

"I know what the eighth vehicle is."

"I'm on my way," Raynes says and hangs up.

In less than an hour, Lin Raynes sits in my kitchen sipping coffee, standard medium roast à la Keurig, and eating what would have been Tiffany's breakfast. His shirt, I swear, is pressed. I've told him about the truck. He doesn't ask me to compare my notes to the list of vehicles driven by my employees. More importantly, he doesn't ask if I'm sure about what I've mentally seen.

According to Raynes, this parked truck may be the first error on the part of the killer. Cars can be traced. I ask if we're sure the truck belongs to the killer. Raynes shrugs and says, "Doesn't matter. We have to check it out." He wants me to immerse myself in the world of orange trucks and see if we can narrow down the make and model. "I'll have a photo array for you later today."

Great, another chunk of time I'll lose.

Raynes is leaving as Tiffany makes her way to the kitchen. I don't know who she's more disconcerted to see. Raynes apologizes and explains why he's here. Tiffany beams. This could be pride. Or sheer delight.

And, of course, she invites him to dinner. The man may as well move in.

* * *

Susan Warrington is standing near my office door when I finally make it in. Marcia asks me without using words if everything is fine.

"Sorry, I'm late," I say to both women. "Car problem." I open the door and usher Susan inside.

She's uncomfortable, an uncommon state. "I don't want to bring this up, and I don't mean to be indelicate, but what do you want to do about a comptroller?"

Dammit. I hadn't planned for this, but I should have. Norm will have to be replaced. I know timing is important. Do it too soon, and we'll seem callous; wait too long, and there will be backlogs of work, and it is budget time.

Perhaps Tiffany is wearing off on me, or I'm getting more adept at handling complicated situations. I have an idea. "What if we asked Faye Bedwell what she thinks? It would be respectful." I'm proud of myself.

Susan doesn't seem as if she likes my suggestion. "That would be very nice." There is more, though, and it makes sense. "But what if it's too much for her? What if she wants us to wait? We are in the middle of the budget process."

My HR director is right. "Let me feel Faye out. Then we can take it from there." What the hell is happening to me?

* * *

I don't have an opportunity to plan my call with Faye and rehearse what I'll say. Norm Bedwell's widow calls me first. She's effusive and grateful. I have no inkling why. It becomes clear as she continues to thank me, adding details with each new offering of gratitude. She thinks I got the Baillies to back off. I move to interject, unsuccessfully. I tell her, more than once, that this was Raynes's doing, not mine. Faye is not buying it. She finally has to stop for breath.

I jump in gently. "On another note, Faye, there is something I would like to ask you."

"Yes."

"We will never forget Norm, but we will need a comptroller." I hesitate.

"Yes. Yes, you do."

"How would you like us to handle this?" I ask her. I ask myself, *What the fuck are you doing?*

"You're kind. Of course, the world needs to go on. You need to go on. Please hire a comptroller. It will help people to heal."

"Speaking of that." I have no idea what I'm about to say. "We'd like to rename the boardroom in honor of Norm. Perhaps a small dedication ceremony. You and Bran could come if you're up to it."

Faye is sniffling. I can almost hear the tears falling. I think this is a good thing. Clearly, I need to make an appointment with my therapist.

* * *

At six o'clock on the dot, our front doorbell rings. Raynes comes bearing gifts. A bouquet of white calla lilies for Tiffany and a honey-processed caturra from Costa Rica. Good choice. Surprising choice. The detective who drinks beer is embarrassed. "I asked Marcia."

I nod and attempt to raise my left eyebrow, but nothing moves.

Tiffany is serving meat. A part of me wishes Raynes would come to dinner every night. She's prepared a delicious coq au vin with a side of butter-drizzled fiddleheads, the edible shoots of the ostrich fern that grow wild in neighboring New Brunswick. It sounds botanically boring. It isn't.

Admittedly, the chicken was raised eating only organic corn from an ancient seed and slept each night next to its cousin, and the fiddleheads were picked and frozen this spring by Tiffany, but the meal is to savour. Both Raynes and I tell her this. She can tell we mean it. She beams.

Dessert does not fare so well. The banana cream pie is neither pie nor creamy but something vegan and unidentifiable. I think the glass pie plate is the only thing that matches its name. But after a good meal, this doesn't matter. Tiffany has opened the coffee bag from Raynes, and it's piping hot.

As per our tradition, Tiffany exits the table at this point. Raynes and I do the dishes. Apparently, it's our time to talk, which we do.

"I have the photo line-up for the trucks," Raynes says. I swear he's playing with the soap bubbles.

"More than happy to help. But I'm not holding out a lot of hope as it was a brief glimpse in a darkish parking lot."

"You never know. We might get lucky."

And we do. In one photo of a Chevrolet Colorado is what appears to be a distended cross. From somewhere in the recesses of my mind, I recognize the cross from the morning Norm died. From that photo, Raynes identifies the manufacturer. The odd colour of the vehicle helps to pinpoint the model. I couldn't remember anything noteworthy about the truck, which Raynes believes may indicate it wasn't old or new. So now, he'll comb through DMV records to see if anyone who owns a truck matching our make and model has a connection to the company or to Norm Bedwell.

"We might hit paydirt," Raynes says. The left eyebrow goes up.

* * *

My phone rings before my alarm goes off. I'm sleeping soundly, perchance dreaming about the Oval Office, and I reach without looking to see who's calling. I should know better. It's Raynes. "It's not even six in the morning." I'm half asleep and fully resentful. "The sun isn't even up."

"The sun is never up in Nova Scotia at this time of the year," Raynes says. "I need to speak to you about a few things. How about coffee and muffins at Starbucks? My treat. Thirty minutes."

Raynes is waiting for me when I arrive 36 minutes later. And his damn cotton t-shirt doesn't have a single wrinkle. I'm convinced my underwear is inside out because I dressed in such a hurry. Two steaming cups and assorted muffins are on the out-of-the-way table. "It's a sundried Ethiopia Sidama." Raynes nods at the coffee.

I can't help but laugh.

He grins. "I asked the clerk."

"Good choice." I mean it. "I'm partial to dark roast."

"Two things." Raynes slides a piece of paper across the table toward me.

"What's that?"

"It's a search warrant."

I stiffen and pull back involuntarily. I wonder if the friendly cop act was a setup all this time. Did I miss a signal somewhere along the line? Was that what all these friendly dinners were about?

Raynes is reaching out in my direction. "It's procedure." It's his way of offering an olive branch for ambushing me at 6:45 in the friggin' morning. "We need to investigate the personal and professional life of every deceased victim. We would normally do this much earlier in the investigation, but the medical examiner has just officially confirmed that Bedwell's death was not by natural causes."

I'm on full alert. I breathe in. Breathe out. Meditation techniques I learned as a kid and continue to practice every day.

Raynes continues to talk. "We'll need to search Bedwell's computer and his files. Anything not connected to the case remains confidential."

"Sh-it." I make it two syllables. Like they do in Alabama.

Raynes covers a grin. "We don't think there's anything to be found, but we have to check."

My heart slows down and my mind stops racing to an imaginary and horrific finish line. Control returns. I continue breathing in for a count of four, holding for a count of four, and exhaling for a count of eight. I think I'm doing this naturally and unobtrusively, but Raynes studies me closely.

I pivot, pretending I hope to appear as if I've been considering the information thrown in my lap in the middle of a Starbucks at the crack of dawn. "Why now?" It is an incoherent question, and I realize this as soon as the words are out of my mouth.

Raynes understands what I'm asking. "We suspected Bedwell's death was murder; however, we had to wait for the official medical examiner's report to get a warrant."

"What did the examiner find?"

Raynes doesn't miss a beat. "I can tell you because coroner's reports are a matter of public record, so you would have access to the information eventually."

I wait for him to continue and continue my meditative breathing.

Raynes makes this sound like a casual conversation between two bros on their way to the hunting lodge. (I have to get back to California.) "It's a little complicated, but when someone deliberately hangs themselves, the ligature marks are different than when forced to hang themselves."

I continue to wait. I can't figure out if I want more information, another minute to recover, or both.

Raynes goes on to explain. "Usually, when people hang themselves, a bruise in the shape of an upside-down V is created. When they are forced to put a noose around their neck, the bruise is more like a straight line."

Now, I'm truly interested, although why eludes me.

Raynes gives me a slight nod. "The difference is because of two factors. One, more force than necessary is often used in homicide strangulation. Second, the victim struggles more, resulting in deep bruises and contusions around the neck. There can even be damage to the inside of the throat, which rarely happens with suicide."

"So, it's confirmed Norm was murdered." The information is obvious, yet I need to hear myself say it to myself. Raynes has worked on this assumption with me for the past few days. Somehow, I must have had a seed of hope that this investigation would not become a major issue. That seed just died.

Now it's back to business. "Of course, I don't mind you gathering whatever you need from Norm's office or the company. We have nothing to hide, but regulators often get nervous when cops visit a cannabis-production facility."

"Do you have to tell them?"

"I do. It's always better to get out in front of these things."

I'm only now realizing that this type of conversation would likely have occurred most often on the premises of the company in question as the warrant is about to be executed. So, the dinners were genuine. "Thanks for the head's up." I mean it. I'm at my best when I'm in control and handling the fallout from the warrant is squarely in my court.

Raynes pauses for the merest beat of a second. There's more. "Once the warrant is executed, it will be in the public domain."

That's intended to mean something to me. Something I'm not going to like. I breathe. Then it hits me. Shi-it. "You mean the media may get hold of this."

The decorated HPD detective nods but doesn't make eye contact. I assume that's embarrassment. "I expect they will. You may want to get out in front of this quickly."

I'm already pushing back my chair. "I'd like to run this by legal first. Then we can get you what you need."

"There's one more thing I shouldn't tell you, but I'm going to anyway."

I brace for more bad news.

"The Baillies' GPS systems don't align."

I'm stunned. "The bullies not only lied, they thought they could get away with it. WTF."

"I thought the same thing. Either they're stupid, or there's a reasonable explanation for why there is more mileage on their cars than there should be according to their travel timeline."

"They're thick but surely not that stupid."

"You'd be amazed," says Raynes.

* * *

My morning has gone to rat crud. Even the Ethiopia Sidama has soured. I'll be on the phone for the next several hours, either trying not to bark orders at an underling or getting a strip ripped off me from on high. There are times I wish anyone else were CEO.

I thank Raynes for breakfast and the heads-up. I hope I sound sincere. Before I buckle my seatbelt, I dial Michael Graves; as usual, he's in the office. I ask him to meet me at mine. "Something has come up."

Michael is waiting for me when I arrive.

I explain about the search warrant as I'm hanging up my coat.

Michael's unruffled. "I anticipated this was coming. Bedwell's office has been draped in crime tape since we found his body. They'll need access to everything behind that crime tape and maybe beyond."

I look at Michael, relieved and annoyed. "I must admit this took me off guard. A head's up would have been nice." So, again this is not Raynes being personal, not an attempt to cut CCC off at the knees.

Before Michael can apologize, I raise a finger.

"No, let me rephrase. A head's up would have been expected."

Michael is uncomfortable and profusely apologetic. Fat lot of good either emotion does me, although I take some small comfort in his discomfort. Ultimately, it hits home that this bombshell is my own doing. I need to pay more attention to what goes on in the office, set clearer expectations, and keep a closer eye on the people under my direct supervision. For a quick second, I wonder if I had done these things earlier would Norm Bedwell be alive? But that is absurd, I reassure myself.

Raynes obviously took his time getting to my office. Fifteen minutes go by before the security buzzer sounds. The coffee shop is only three minutes away, and that is if you're driving at a snail's pace. Michael and I let the police detective inside.

Michael is all business as usual. He scans the warrant and nods "yes'" in my direction.

I wave Raynes forward. "My forensics team is on their way," he says.

Of course, they are. Goddammit.

I have not been in Bedwell's office since the morning I found him. It is the same as I remember it and simultaneously as if I had never stepped foot in his room.

The thick manila rope dangles from the ceiling. The noose gapes about two feet in front of the mahogany desk, almost as if framing Norm's face in one of his favorite places. Norm loved that desk despite its pockmarks and pits. A piece of family furniture from way back, he once told me with a mouth full of danish. Below the noose is a stain on the beige and green rug that takes up much of the office. The fluid is clear, not the color of blood.

"The paramedics worked to resuscitate him, even though they knew it was too late." Raynes answers my unasked question. I wasn't even aware the detective stood beside me.

My gaze falls on the framed picture of dogs playing poker, a conversation piece. Norm loved it, a joke gift from coworkers when he left his last job. I wonder if he felt as welcomed here. I make a mental note to review how we celebrate employees and make them feel part of the corporate culture.

Norm's computer case is on a side table in front of stacks of paper. It must be budget material. A standard-issue chair, black webbed with armrests, a dipped back, and straight stainless steel legs, is in front of the table. Its companion sits a few feet in front of the noose. I assume this was the chair Norm stood on or was forced to stand on.

The computer, the pièce de résistance for the HPD, is positioned squarely in the middle of Norm's desk. I wonder if it's on and suddenly realize Raynes is speaking.

"If it's all right with you, we'll station a patrol officer outside while we remove everything we need." Not a request. Raynes continues without interruption, "We'll try to get everything back as soon as possible, and anything unrelated to the investigation remains confidential."

"IT will have passwords if you need them," Michael says. "Just call me if you do."

"Is the phone personal?" Raynes points to the iPhone on Norm's mahogany desk.

"Not unless Norm made a special request to use his own phone for business," I answer. "I'll check with Neela to confirm, but I doubt it."

Raynes takes the phone and puts it in an evidence bag. He turns to Michael and reiterates the reason for the later invasion of our collective office space. "We'd usually have done all this much earlier, but in this case, we initially thought we were dealing with a suicide and needed to confirm otherwise before proceeding."

Michael nods and says something lawyerly. The timing makes sense, and in the end, the timing doesn't matter. In the bustle of uniformed activity and Raynes's continued explanations for the HPD presence, I miss Susan Warrington's attempt at entering.

She looks at me accusingly from the other side of the police tape. "What's going on?"

I detect a tone and don't like it.

Raynes interjects. "We're executing a search warrant. We'll need you to stay outside the office for the next few hours."

"Why aren't they outside?" She nods brusquely in my direction and Michael's.

"One is legal counsel; the other is the authorized owner of the premises." Raynes is perfunctory. He turns away.

"There may be proprietary information on that computer." Susan points to Norm's laptop, not letting go of the tone.

"We've already covered that." I turn to leave the room. "If you need anything, Michael will be pleased to help," I say to Raynes. I brush past Warrington and continue down the hall to my office. I'm aware she's humpfing behind me. But there is something I'm missing, something not quite right.

* * *

Susan gets thwarted in her attempt to enter my office in my wake. From somewhere, Marcia has materialized. "You have a call waiting," she says to me, then

126

turns to Susan. "I can set up a time for you to meet."

There is no call waiting. I know that before I enter the room. The tactic is quintessential Marcia. She's protecting me, alerting me to an issue I'll need to attend to, or both.

In this case, it's both. "A reporter from the Canada Cable Network called." Marcia's tone neutral. "She wants you to get back to her as soon as possible. I told her you were tied up in meetings all day."

God bless Marcia. She has given me a day to prep. "Can you call Thorne and see if he's available?" Thorne Tannehill is a local communications consultant who specializes in media relations. We've used him before, when we announced the formation of the company, in preparation for our official opening, and throughout the controversy that clung to the federal government's announcement that recreational cannabis would be legal in Canada.

"I'll ask him to come in for 11 o'clock." The implication is clear: Thorne will be here.

I can't believe it's still morning. It feels like I've been here for days. I reach for the phone.

David Clements answers on the second ring. "What's up?" he asks before I can even say hello. Clearly my regulator is not screening out my calls. That's rarely good news.

"I wanted to let you know that the Halifax Police Department is here executing a search warrant for Norm Bedwell's office. They are concerned his death may be the result of foul play."

My pronouncement is met with silence. It travels down the fibre optic network through my cell phone and into my office. I know most people feel an obligation to fill the silence. I don't. Nonetheless, I think it prudent to add a few mollifying details. "No reason to suspect Norm's death is related to his job, but the police must do their due diligence. Anything uncovered during the investigation that is irrelevant to his death, including company information, will be kept confidential."

More silence. Finally, David says, "Well, this is certainly a chunderfuck."

I have no idea what that means, but I couldn't agree more.

Chapter 7

I've managed to pacify David Clements.

Controversy in the weed industry is standard operating procedure, so he's used to having crap land in his lap. Murder is well outside the ordinary. Fortunately, I got the sense from David that he believed me when I said Norm's death is unlikely linked to anything happening at CCC. We have a good reputation and are a key player in the country's cannabis sector. Prior to opening the production facility in Nova Scotia, we were licensed to provide medical marijuana for those with a prescription, so we're a known entity.

I promised to keep David in the loop.

"No surprises, Riel," David cautioned. "I can tolerate getting bad news. I cannot tolerate finding out from a third party that there is a problem or finding out too late that I need to fix said problem."

Warning received. Now on to the next fire. I'm about to ask Michael for an update when CCC's legal counsel knocks on my door as if hearing my unspoken clarion call. He's plucking at his left eyebrow. What is it about Nova Scotians and their eyebrows?

"They're gone," he says, as if that answers all my questions. Michael looks at my face and sees right away the summary is insufficient. He continues. "The police have packaged up everything they want to examine more closely, including Norm's phone and computer. We have receipts for everything removed.

"They also gave the office a more thorough search and forensic detailing, although hair, fiber, and fingerprints will likely do them no good. Too much of everything and, unless someone doesn't belong here, the evidence can be explained away."

"You think someone we know did this?" I'm a little shocked.

"I think someone Norm knew did this. We should prepare for that. You might ask Thorne to start drafting possible statements, good news and bad."

Now I have an urge to pluck an eyebrow, any eyebrow. "Thorne's on his way in," I say absently.

A somewhat singsong voice announces, "I'm already here." Thorne strides in, tall and slim, prematurely grey, with a large swatch of purple running from the crown of his head to the tip of his bangs, which he constantly shoves off his forehead. The outfit today is downplayed funk. He has a linen totem shirt that somehow refuses to wrinkle. The jeans are rolled at the cuff, and the blue deerskin sneakers are frayed enough to be cool.

Thorne is 99 percent confidence and one percent show, a winning combination. Marcia walks in as Thorne settles into a chair at the table to the left of my desk.

She has that look and points toward my phone. "Senator Williams is on your private line."

Say no more. Thorne is already gathering up paper and files. "I'll meet you in the conference room."

Breathe in. Breathe out. I give myself 15 seconds to prepare for what I'm sure will be more uncomfortable than an enema.

When I pick up the line, John doesn't say "hello" or "how are you" or anything remotely conversational. "I expect a call when shit hits the fan." The tone is calm, almost pleasant.

"You were next on my list," I assure him.

"I should have been on your list before you called David Clements." The tone turns less friendly.

No excuse will appease his anger. If I say it was a crazy morning, that implies I can't handle disruption and upheaval, cornerstones of any CEO, not to mention a presidential candidate. If I say I have a legal obligation to call the regulator first, then I don't know how to play the game properly. If I say David called me, the lie will be discovered within minutes. There is nothing to do but apologize and assure the Democratic senator from Santa Barbara that it will not happen again.

"What in God's green earth is going on up there?"

I fill John in on the warrant, the search, the possible evidence, the media call, and Thorne's presence.

"Why the hell do you use that man?" he snaps. "I could have Sara Beth on Zoom in minutes."

Sara Beth Calhoun is the senator's go-to person for all things media. She's savvy, experienced, breathes media, and she's American. However, what works south of the 49th parallel, does not work in Nova Scotia or Canada. I need someone who knows how local media operates. I need Thorne, but I don't bother explaining this to my father-in-law. We've already had this discussion on several occasions.

"Keep me posted," John says when it's clear I'm not rising to the bait. "And clean up this chunderfuck."

So, David Clements called the senator directly after we spoke.

* * *

Thorne has coffee and a raft of paper spread out in front of him by the time I arrive in the conference room. "This isn't going to be easy, but you have several choices."

He lays them out for me. Option one, say we can't speak about an issue currently under investigation by the police, a common tactic for matters before the court but used less often mid-investigation. On the pro side, I'll evade or avoid answering difficult questions. On the downside, it may and most likely will appear as if we have something to hide. It also will not stop others from speaking about the issue, even if they are not informed or knowledgeable. God, I hate the media.

Another option is to be upfront and answer questions from reporters, no matter how tricky. Thorne can help me prepare responses to deflect and bridge back to my key messages. The advantage here is that we appear accessible, open, and forthright, if I do my job well. The disadvantage is until we know who killed Norm Bedwell, I can't honestly say the company had no involvement.

Then there is a middle ground. Say we will help in any way we can but alert reporters in advance to the fact that we can't speak about matters directly related to the police investigation while it's under way. It's limbo land, giving us neither the distinct disadvantages nor advantages of the first two options.

We pick door number three. It will require more tap dancing, but it will also let me see how the media play this out and potentially douse any flames before they become a raging fire.

Thorne starts drafting a list of possible questions the media may ask. These are, as usual, written in a blunt, often confrontational tone as if reporters were asking them live on television. The first question sets the tone: How did a murderer get inside your offices in the first place?

The media likes straightforward answers, black and white. Most answers, however, as in this case, are grey. I can and will talk about the security measures we take to ensure the safety of employees, visitors, and the community. I can and will point out that the administrative offices, while physically attached to the grow-op, are separate from that facility. You cannot move from the former to the latter without going outside and entering through a different, far-more-secure entryway. It's about reassuring critics that cannabis production is safe and that we are not routinely tossing drugs into a garbage can for kids to rifle through. Admittedly, the safety spiel is a harder sell when someone gets murdered on your premises.

Thorne and I spend the next three hours coming up with possible questions and acceptable answers. I know he thinks I'm ready when he gathers the papers in front of him. "Do you want me there during the interviews?"

I tell him I think that will appear too PR(ish). Thorne nods in agreement.

"Keep it casual, not informal, but relaxed because you have nothing to hide. Don't wear a tie, and for god's sake, don't roll up your sleeves."

* * *

I return the reporter's call at the end of the day and go through the main news line, not her cell. That will buy me some time, and it does. I receive a voicemail, leave a message simply saying I am returning her call, and give Marcia's number. We can play telephone tag for several hours if not days, as intended.

That doesn't mean the story isn't the lead on the six o'clock news. Tiffany and I are seated in the family room downstairs, sipping a glass of chardonnay and waiting for the ax to drop. She's being supportive. I'm wondering how long it will take the senator to call.

Zahra Bashir is covering the story for CCN, the country's national cable news station. Thorne has already given me the rundown on her: she's experienced, persistent, intelligent, and fair.

Tonight, she stands in front of the camera; she is wearing her serious expression. Her black hijab, with its burgundy border, reaffirms the solemnity of the situation. Raynes brushes her off politely but firmly, only confirming that the police are

135

investigating a death at the Canadian Cannabis Corp. Next up, Neil Phillips.

I cringe. Tiffany does the same. This guy is a pain in the cannabis industry's side. He has fought the legalization of marijuana in this country since pretty boy prime minister, Justin Trudeau, announced it would happen.

Phillips has amassed quite a following. The hero worship is, in part, due to his appearance. As executive director of a national right-wing think tank, Phillips comes with professional credibility, complemented by attractive features, not ruggedly handsome, but tall, fit, and well-coifed. Phillips comes armed with medical evidence, some scientific, and most pseudo-science. He also has a cadre of middle-class Canadians who can step forward at the drop of a hat to express concerns about their children's safety.

The murder of Bedwell is like Christmas day for him. He explains to Bashir that it's precisely the kind of situation he and his followers forewarned. Where there is weed, there is evil. Obviously, I'm paraphrasing, but that was the man's main message. Then again, he only has one.

As usual, Phillips's message hits home. My cell phone rings the instant Bashir signs off. So does the landline. I take Thorne's call. Tiffany says hello to her father.

* * *

Zahra Bashir calls me directly on my personal cell phone at 8:30 the next morning, proving that she's good at her job. If she can unearth my cell number, what else can she dig up? I agree to an interview at 11:00 but put parameters around the questions I would be able to answer. She consents, but I don't believe her. She doesn't expect me to.

In anticipation of the TV interview, I dress accordingly: a long-sleeve royal blue shirt with buttoned cuffs, navy pants, and loafers. The intent is to appear casual and authoritative and to exude confidence without arrogance and stiffness. Marcia nods her approval when she arrives in the office, so I know I'm good on the appearance front.

Michael Graves shows up to run through the legal issues: what I cannot say without violating some legislative tenet. He's plucking at his eyebrow again. Susan Warrington is more controlled but equally concerned. She focuses on ensuring the staff doesn't feel like the CEO is pointing the finger of blame in their direction. We opt to go through a few practice questions later to reassure her.

"Thank you." She stands up to leave. "And good luck." Susan absently reaches out to straighten the coaster and coffee cup on my desk.

"Anything else?" I sense there is more to follow.

Susan hesitates. "Have you been in touch with Faye Bedwell lately?"

Dammit. The wife. I lean my head to the left.

Susan adds, "I think it would be a sign of respect to let Faye know you are getting interviewed and that we would like to acknowledge how much Norm meant to the company publicly."

"I'll call her now," I say, reaching for the phone. Faye has given me all her numbers: landline, cell, and work. I assume she's at her office, and she is. As always, Faye is grateful for whatever crumb we toss her way. That sounds mean, I know. But I am always amazed at how much people need other people. She's delighted I called to let her know about the interview (thank you, Susan) and even more delighted we want to honor Norm in some small way. I caution her that the thank you may be edited in the television version but definitely will be part of my remarks.

Bashir is prompt by my definition: she shows up 10 minutes early. Clearly, this will be a lead story. A camera operator is with her. More and more of the broadcast interviews I do are by reporters who also work the camera. She asks if it's okay to set up and makes small talk while the wires, lights, and angles all get professional attention.

Now she's ready. I hope I am.

Bashir's first question is intended to relax me, perhaps even to get me off guard. She wants to know what has happened at the Canadian Cannabis Corp.

"Our comptroller Norman Bedwell was found deceased in his office." My tone is neutral. "We called the police, and they are investigating."

Bashir dives in. She asks about the details of the crime.

I ignore the question. "On behalf of all of us at CCC, I want to extend our deepest condolences to the Bedwell family. Norm was admired and respected by everyone. We miss him."

Not to be deterred by my pre-planned humanity, Bashir continues probing for particulars, and I respond, "As I mentioned before the interview, we are unable to talk about the matter while the police are investigating it." I give the camera my best sorry-I-can't-be-more-help expression. "We want to let the police do their work and have the greatest faith they will find the answers we all need."

"Could it have been someone who works at the company?" Bashir is slightly more insistent.

Now I can repeat my previous answer, but that may imply it is an employee, which is Susan's concern. "I can't speak about the police investigation, but I have the highest respect for our employees and their work. They are an exceptional group of people."

Bashir hesitates for just a second, perhaps realizing I'm media trained. She's unlikely to pressure me into a slip, especially since I prepped for the interview. She pivots. "The murder raises issues of access and security. How do you address those? People want to know how a murderer got inside your company. Your cannabis business."

I struggle not to flinch at the repeated use of the word "murder" and its derivatives. I also attempt not to rise to Bashir's confrontational tone. News items that aren't live rarely include the interviewer's questions, just the interviewee's responses. I need to appear calm and reasonable.

"Security is a priority for our company." I'm on comfortable ground now. "There is a three-level entry system to access the production plant. The administration office, which is separate from the plant, has a camera system and secure entry. We review security protocols monthly."

"And yet you are the first cannabis company in the country to have a murder on the premises." Bashir waits a second before she smiles.

Sonofabitch.

* * *

My day goes downhill from here. I give the Senator and Clements, in that order, a head's up about the interview and how it will likely end. My father-in-law reiterates that I should have used Sara Beth. There is no appropriate response. If I say "yes," it indicates I make bad decisions. If I say "no," it shows I'm not good with media, no matter the prepping. I tell him and Clements that a video file of the interview is on its way. At least they'll get the whole story.

I settle into my day, but the routine has gotten sucked out of me. I'm on edge, uncertain about my next steps and expectations, two states that never sit well with me. I shuffle some papers, click on a few emails, pick up the phone and set it down. I'm no longer sure if I need a distraction or need to get away from all the distractions that have popped up in the last few weeks.

Shortly after lunch, a chickpea and avocado salad sandwich that I grabbed from the fridge in a moment of weakness this morning, Marcia knocks and says she received a call from Detective Raynes. He'd like to come by later today. We're both nonplussed.

Why would Raynes not call me directly?

Marcia, as is her way, gives me a few seconds to process. "He suggested Michael Graves be at the meeting and Susan Warrington."

So, more crap is about to hit the fan. We set the meeting for 2:30. Time enough for the four of us to sit down, for me to debrief the CCC team and arrive home in time for Bashir to end my day on another upbeat note.

Raynes walks in on time. No smile. More of a chagrined look, which is a first. I want to take a photo, but I'm sure that will be considered rude. I'm behind my desk, Susan and Michael to my left, which leaves Raynes on his own in right field.

"I appreciate you're taking the time out of your busy schedules," Raynes says, albeit tritely, as he settles into the appointed chair. "We have an issue we need to discuss. Before we have that discussion, I will need your assurance that what we talk about in this room will go no further, at least not until the police investigation concludes."

We all nod our acceptance, ill at ease and likely lying through our teeth. "We have not completed our forensic audit, but it appears Mr. Bedwell had identified a potential theft within the company."

We all sit a little straighter, leaning in. If true and the theft is significant, this could be a disaster for CCC. That kind of thing will have Neil Phillips and his followers dancing in the streets.

Before we can express disbelief or outrage, Raynes shuts us down with a simple downward movement of his right hand. "What we're seeing is not significant from a narcotics or revenue point of view, but it could be a motive for murder."

I am ramrod tight and stiff. I breathe to relax the muscles and do rapid body scan. The few seconds inward help outwardly. "Exactly what are we dealing with?" I am calm and back in control.

"To be honest, we don't know." Raynes looks me in the eye for the first time. "Bedwell had an encrypted file on his laptop that contained production volumes, seed purchases, and plant disposal. Even being generous, there is an unexplained discrepancy between what CCC produces and what goes out the door for sale."

"You're saying someone is skimming off the floor," Michael says.

"Yes," Raynes responds simply. "It's not a large quantity, but it is large enough to be noticed. From a police perspective, this usually indicates someone has a small side business selling weed."

Cannabis production works like this: companies develop strains that they sell as seeds or even buds to production companies such as CCC. We, in turn, transform the seeds into healthy plants that are dried and can also have oil extracted from them. This final product is sold legally in Canada and certain U.S. states in approved retail outlets and online for medical purposes, CCC's primary business until Justin Trudeau opened the floodgates for recreational cannabis.

Like any seed or plant, there is no guarantee a healthy bloom results. Plants die, they're dropped, someone forgets to reset the thermostat software and the room gets too cold or too dry. We build in a 10 percent loss and have been consistent, give or take a little on that number. Shit.

"Someone is skimming one to two percent a month?" I ask.

"It seems that way," Raynes says.

No one will become a billionaire at that low rate, but it will, over time, be enough to buy a nice boat, a bigger home, a cottage on a lake, or a vacation to Greece. All four actually. And there will always be a market for our product. Even though marijuana is legal in Canada, prices at retail outlets, whether run by the government or private companies, are steep. Many regular users opt to buy from street dealers at lower prices.

"Do you know who is doing this?" Susan asks.

"No idea," says Raynes. "That's why I'm here."

"It has to be someone inside and closely connected to the plants." I'm talking more to myself than the others in the room.

"What makes you think that?" Raynes asks.

"Someone is walking out of here with seeds or plants. Or both. They must know how to stay out of the camera's view and get the product to their car." I am speaking primarily to myself once again. "That means they need to work early or late hours when few people are around, or they need to have a job developing plant strains or testing soils or something that means it's commonplace to see them with pots of weed."

Everyone nods their agreement. We're all thinking the problem through. I've even forgotten to be angry at Raynes, although I'm not sure why I was so upset with him. "How many people would fall into that category?" Raynes asks.

"Not many," I say. "Production manager, master grower, and quality assurance team. Budmasters would have easy access to the plants, but I can't see how they could get them out unless they're smuggling one plant out at a time."

"That might work given the scale we're talking about," says Raynes.

"So that gives us roughly 10 people who could do this," Susan notes. "I can get you names."

Raynes nods his appreciation.

I'm thinking that there's something we're missing. "Do you have the numbers?"

Raynes picks up on what I'm doing. "Something not right?"

"I don't know. Maybe."

The detective hands me a sheet of paper, and I scan the numbers on it. He gives copies to Michael and Susan. Production volumes are down by about two percent overall, seed purchases are up half of that, and plant disposal is roughly consistent. "It works like this," I say, still more to myself than the others. "I pick a few plants to smuggle out of CCC. I slide them into my backpack when I'm out of camera range and no one is paying attention. Then I exit the building."

"Because no one will miss one or two plants." Raynes continues my thread.

"We certainly won't miss them at that level, but one or two plants every time should raise alarm bells," I respond.

"It did – with Norm," Michael points out.

"He's the freakin' comptroller." I struggle to control my frustration. "The production manager should pick up on this. I should pick up on this." Blame is not second nature to me. It doesn't tend to solve problems or enhance progress. Responsibility is another issue, and I take mine seriously as well as those around me.

I check the numbers again. And there it is. Right in front of me. Sonofabitch.

"Figured it out, eh," Raynes says. I swear the man smiled.

"It's disposal." Everyone looks at me for further clarification. "We pay attention to containers coming into the plant. We pay attention to plants in our growth op. We don't give a shit about the ones that don't make it."

"So, no one's watching." Raynes nods.

"Worse than that," I say. "If you're loading the disposal cart, I doubt anyone is questioning what you're putting on it. Healthy and unhealthy plants can appear the same, especially from a distance. Then once you hit disposal out back, it's out of sight, out of mind. Even if someone questioned what you were doing before then, it would be simple enough to say you made an honest mistake putting a healthy plant in the disposal cart."

"How would someone get the plants off the premises entirely?" Raynes asks.

"They could drive around back and unload the roll-off dumpster where the plants get placed for pick-up, but you'd need an access key to get into the area from outside the plant. Repeated unwarranted access should raise alarm bells with IT."

"How are the plants disposed?"

"We contract that out," I explain. "Under federal law, all unused or unsold plants must be destroyed."

"That means no one is going to question an access code from the disposal company," Raynes says. It's not a question.

"Sonofabitch," we both say at the same time.

Susan is already checking something on her laptop. "We have two budmasters responsible for ongoing disposal. Clay Brandt and Gus Whittaker."

Raynes glances in my direction.

I shrug. I don't know either person.

"The production company is Superior Haul," Susan continues.

"How can we fix this?" Michael asks.

"Right off the top, we should install cameras in the disposal area and barcode all plants as soon as they enter the facility, not when they are shipped for sale. That way, we always have a digital trail. But let's take a minute to think this through," I add. "I'll ask Marcia to add the issue to the agenda for the next management meeting. In the meantime, let's get IT in here ASAP to update them. Michael, you'll also need to connect with Lucy Chen. I'm sure there is a compliance concern erupting here."

Raynes raises a finger. "I know you need to fix this, but I need to catch a murderer. I don't want to alert anyone we're on to them."

Fair enough. "How do you want to work this?" I ask.

"My guess is whoever is doing this saw an opportunity and went for it. I doubt we're dealing with a seasoned criminal. Chances are they'll crack in interrogation. If not, we can get a search warrant for both of their homes once we have more evidence. Are they currently at work?" Raynes asks.

"Budmasters work different shifts," I explain. "That way, there is always a plant expert on site."

Susan turns back to her keyboard. "Gus is on days this week."

"Okay to interview him in your office now?" Raynes asks as his left brow raises.

Why the hell not? See how well we're doing so far. I'm sure the company can run itself.

* * *

We decide the best way to draw Gus in without waving a gigantic red flag is to have his boss, Gordon Howell, ask him to come to my office to meet a potential new supplier. That is relatively commonplace, but usually, the meeting is between the budmaster and the supplier. I let Gordon know it's a local company the government requested us to meet. Such political requests for favors are not uncommon.

Fifteen minutes later, Gus sits in my office. He's a tall, Black man with close-cropped hair, an impressive beard, and dressed in budmaster fashion: blue jeans, long-sleeved blue tee, and taupe work boots. Gus takes one look at Raynes and knows something is up.

This awareness doesn't get lost on Raynes. "Sorry to get you here under false pretenses, but we needed to speak with you."

"What's up?" Gus appears nervous, but who wouldn't be?

Raynes glances in my direction. "The police have discovered that CCC is losing product on a regular basis."

"We'd notice that." Gus shakes his head "no," then sits straighter and leans in. "With our protocols, we'd catch that right away."

"You might not in this quantity." Raynes's eyes never leave Gus's face.

"How much are we talking?" Gus asks.

"About 2,300 grams a week," says Raynes. In U.S. terms, that's about five pounds, but most countries, like Canada, use the metric system.

Gus lifts his chin, and his brows pull together as if mentally calculating the product loss. "That means someone is stealing five or six plants a week." He glances our way for confirmation. Raynes nods. Gus laughs. "I'll be damned. Someone has a side business."

Gus has been so intent on staring at the HPD detective that he has forgotten the company's CEO is also in the room.

"How could someone have a side business with our protocols?" My tone makes it clear I don't find this amusing.

"Damned if I know," says Gus, apparently unphased by my CEO status. "We go over the security requirements on a regular basis. We even have 'theft week.'"

Raynes raises his left eyebrow. "What the hell is 'theft week'?"

"We ask employees in the plant to do their best to steal product, plants, seeds, packaged goods," explains Gus. "Anyone who can get out the door with contraband gets a day off, and we tighten security. But no one has ever gotten out the door with anything," he notes, "and believe me, they've tried."

I feel Raynes's eyes on me. He barely moves his chin.

Like I know what the hell that means. "Will you keep your eye out?" I ask. "Please keep this conversation confidential, only between the three of us."

Gus stands, ready to leave. "I'll take tonight and see if I can figure out how someone could do this. Most of our security focuses on preventing theft for personal use or outright robbery. The small-time side business wasn't on our radar."

Once Gus is gone, Raynes smiles. "Glad you read my signal correctly. I don't think Whittaker had any idea this was happening, but we'll investigate his spending habits. If necessary, we'll do a second interview. That one won't be as pleasant."

"Shift changes at 4:30," I say, surprising myself. Apparently, my mouth works separately from my mind now. "Clay Brandt will replace Gus then. Do you want to talk to him?"

Raynes glances at his watch. "That gives us time for a quick coffee." He slaps my shoulder.

Good grief, what is happening to me?

* * *

Clay Brandt is almost the polar opposite of Gus Whittacker. Where Gus is tall and hirsute, Clay doesn't top 5'7" and has a perfectly shaven head. He is very muscular and certainly works out regularly. While Gus is more reserved and thoughtful, Clay is confidently extroverted. What he shares with his fellow budmaster is the ability to read the room, at least this room. Unlike Gus, however, Clay doesn't acknowledge the trap he finds himself in.

"How can I help?" He turns to me first, then Raynes. At least he got the pecking order right.

I introduce Raynes as the detective investigating Norm Bedwell's death. Clay feigns shock, or maybe he's truly shocked. He may never have seen Raynes before. "We've identified a problem we're hoping you can help us solve," I say assuming the script will play out as it did in act one.

Either Clay isn't as quick as Gus, or he doesn't want to let us in. Once I've explained the situation, he chafes. "We run regular drills. I'm telling you, no one could get product out of this plant without being detected. And who the hell would want five pounds of weed a week? Anyone that doped up would be spotted a mile away."

The use of "pounds" gives him away. Clay is American, which is not unusual in this business. Canada doesn't have many budmasters, because until it legalized weed, there were few places for them to work outside of the medical cannabis sector. Once recreational cannabis outlets opened on every street corner, however, companies like CCC cast a net far and wide for experts.

"Do you know why someone would want to risk their job and a jail stint to steal that much or that little weed?" Raynes asks. I wonder if there is an implied threat.

Clay seems to think so. At least his flashing eyes indicate he does, but he resists the urge to snap back. "No, sir." He smartly leaves it at that.

Raynes's chin moves microscopically.

I know the drill. Once Clay exits, I look at Raynes quizzically. "Did you get something out of that?"

"It's not what he said that interests me. It's what he didn't. He doesn't ask us how we know product is missing, yet denies it is possible, and he doesn't offer to help."

"Now, how do you turn supposition into evidence?"

"We don't have enough for a search warrant, and to be frank, it's better for you if it doesn't come to that." I make a mental note to figure out why a search warrant is not good for me. "I'd prefer an admission of guilt. I'll start with a review of both their financials, and now, since they are both persons of interest, I can check with the DMV to see what they drive. Can you hold off making any changes to the disposal area until I have that information?"

I agree to Raynes's request. The truth is the amount of stolen product doesn't hurt our bottom line. It's an optics issue. We don't want to be the cannabis company that has lax security. To quote my father-in-law quoting my regulator, that would be a chunderfuck.

And that would be why I don't want Raynes to execute a search warrant.

* * *

Tiffany can tell when I'm having an off day from the second I open the front door and sometimes sooner. "What's wrong?" she asks as I enter the kitchen. I can hear the concern in her voice. It always amazes me that she cares and that she cares about me. I don't love this woman, but if I were to die for anyone in this world, it would be her. I respect loyalty.

I fill her in on my day. Her hand reaches for my arm, a gesture of comfort. But her eyes don't meet mine. That I did not expect. "You'll have to call," Tiffany says quietly.

Dammit. I phone the senator before I have a glass of wine or a minute to unwind. To say that he is not pleased with his son-in-law is an understatement. It's no longer about me but about the possibility of political fallout. John Williams's connection to cannabis is well known, but the emphasis has always been on the medical side of things, even though weed is legal in his state. There is a Neil Phillips in every jurisdiction where cannabis is legal.

To his credit, John is less of a ranter and more of a fixer. "Bring in an auditor right away. Let's demonstrate we are committed to getting to the bottom of this. Let's show the government and the community that we put security above all else. I'll have names for you by tomorrow morning."

I'm glad I talked to John first. Now I have an action plan I can share with the regulator. It's an hour earlier in Ottawa, so I catch David Clements just as he is about to leave for the day. I explain the situation and the solution.

Technically, cannabis regulators don't tell me how to run my business; they only get to say when we have broken a specific regulation or law. A lapse in security might or might not fall under their purview. But it doesn't matter. You don't want regulators as enemies because they can make life miserable.

Clements is brief. "Keep me posted." I have no idea how to interpret that.

I'm looking forward to a cup of decaf Tarrazu coffee from Costa Rica via Vocanica Coffee in Georgia. Fittingly, a thank you from my father-in-law for some glad-handing I did for him last year. As the French press is settling, it occurs to me that I have one more call to make. I can't believe Tiffany didn't suggest it.

Raynes sounds like he was expecting my call, as if we regularly phone each other to chat. I explain the situation and ask if it compromises his investigation. It doesn't since the auditor will conduct the review either offsite, preferably, or in the admin offices.

As I'm ending the call, Tiffany walks in. "Who was that?"

"Raynes."

My wife beams.

Chapter 8

The six o'clock news offers up only leftovers from the day before. Evidently Bashir can't dig up any new information, so Neil Phillips makes a repeat appearance. He intones his dangers-of-cannabis mantra and branches out to throw shade on the HPD. I wonder what Raynes will think. The follow-up, third in the news line-up, isn't enough to add fuel to the existing fire, but the fact the story has any legs is more than enough to worry senators and regulators alike.

I do not sleep well. I have these periods. I'm not worried about what people will think of me but how those thoughts can affect the future of my career. At 5 a.m., I give up. I shower, dress, and eat a yogurt and granola parfait that Tiffany prepares for herself the night before. She always makes an extra one for me, just in case. I'm out the door by 5:35 a.m.

The parking lot, as usual, is almost empty. It's a large lot; we need space at the front (and back) for delivery trucks. I walk toward the front gate, counting one black SUV, one silver SUV, one four-door sedan, and maybe a Camry. It's my mantra. Screw you, Neil Phillips.

I am running my card across the security reader when I see it. Orange truck far right tucked almost out of sight. I'm uncertain what to do at this point or what's expected of me. I always play by the rules, yet I almost sprint back to my car. Somehow my cell phone is in my hand, and I'm dialing Raynes.

"We have got to stop meeting like this." I hear the laughter in his voice.

"Orange truck." I'm almost gasping, moving so quickly back to my car.

"Where?" Raynes doesn't miss a beat. I can hear him scrambling to put clothes on in the background.

"It's in the parking lot. Empty," I say, anticipating his next question.

"I'm on my way. Stay put."

Well, so much for Raynes's rules. After a few minutes, I get out of my Lexus and casually saunter over to the truck. There's nothing casual about how I'm feeling. I keep glancing around, expecting someone to jump out of the darkness at any moment. And somehow, I continue moving forward. It's the scene in every horror movie when audiences yell, "Don't go there."

I snap a picture of the truck's license plate and all sides of the vehicle. I even get several pictures of the inside from the driver's side and the passenger's side. Each snap, whirr, click is preceded by a furtive glance around the lot. It remains empty. I head back to my car and climb in, wishing I had stopped for coffee. Even a McDonald's would taste good right about now. And in fairness to the Golden Arches, the coffee is very decent.

Turns out, it may be just as well I don't have any liquid to spill. A lone figure approaches the truck. I feel myself stiffen and straighten, and then I immediately slide down in my seat. I've watched enough *Law & Order* to know what pretend cops do. Raynes is at least 10 minutes out. I'm staying hidden while simultaneously getting a description of the perp (perhaps I watch too much *Law & Order*) by taking his picture. It is a man.

He is now in the truck and slowly backing out of the CCC parking lot. I turn my car on and follow. I honestly don't know what the hell is wrong with me lately.

I call Raynes to update him. There is little traffic on the road, so it's easy to keep the orange truck in sight without appearing to be a stalker. At least, I think so. I can tell Raynes is conflicted because a civilian shouldn't tail a potential killer. On the other hand, he doesn't want to lose the opportunity to nab the orange truck. Yep, definitely too much cop TV.

It's a dilemma the driver solves for us when he turns into the Enfield Lumber Yard, a long-time, well-respected business in the community. It's a typical lumberyard: brightly lit, busy, noisy, and dusty. Buddy, as Nova Scotians like to call those with no known name, gets out of his truck. He's in no hurry as he grabs a lunch pail and makes his way toward the main office.

I damn near jump out of my skin when Raynes knocks on my window a few seconds later. He must have flown here. I point to the tall, slim man with the lunch pail. Raynes quickly makes his way to Buddy, and I follow, having no idea why.

Buddy is inside saying hello to someone behind the front counter when Raynes catches up with him. He turns when Raynes yells, "Sir!"

The man, I'm now calling PK for Potential Killer, is both startled and afraid. Raynes does not have his gun out, but it is visible. Nova Scotians are reeling from a mass shooting earlier this year, the worst in the history of the country, that has left a scar on the province. Raynes is smart enough to reach for his shield first (I learned that lingo from *Law & Order*). PK and the woman behind the counter visibly relax, then stiffen. The gunman in the mass shooting dressed as an RCMP officer and drove what appeared to be an RCMP vehicle.

Raynes can read their minds. "I'm Detective Lin Raynes with the Halifax Police Department. Shield number 6483. You can confirm with 911."

The woman behind the counter reaches for the phone. If she is afraid of us, she is hiding it remarkably well. It takes less than a minute for her to turn to Raynes and smile. "How can we help you, officer?"

I'm tempted to correct her. It should be "detective," but it doesn't seem to bother Raynes. "I need to speak with you." He looks at PK. "Is there someplace we can talk in private?"

The obviously curious and nameless woman behind the counter tells us the meeting room is free. PK leads the way. I follow. Raynes turns to me. "What part of 'stay in the car' did you not understand?"

I don't even have time to feign confusion as we're already at the meeting room.

PK ushers us inside. He seems more curious than concerned. "What can I do for you officer?"

This time Raynes doesn't let it slide. He corrects PK, and his tone is not friendly. It's also not unfriendly. "The orange truck outside." I slide the paper I've written the plate number on toward Raynes. "Licence CFW 298. Is that yours?"

PK nods.

"Could I please see some identification?" Raynes asks. It's not a question.

And now PK has a name: Sean Gillis. His driver's license is current, although his photo does not do him justice. Sean easily tops six feet and is lanky and athletic. He has a head of thick black hair that he has worked some magic with styling mousse and gel. Not a single hair moves, yet he has a natural wind-blown look.

As I'm admiring Sean's hairstyling artistry, Raynes calls the office to confirm the Chevrolet Colorado is registered in his name and there are no outstanding warrants. So far, Sean is getting straight A's. "Were you parked this morning in the lot at the Canadian Cannabis Corp.?"

Sean launches an apology. He didn't realize he couldn't park there or didn't think he was hurting anyone. After all, the lot is mostly empty.

Raynes lets him ramble on. I assume he's assessing something about the man's demeanor, whatever that might be. The guy sounds genuinely confused and contrite, but I often misread people's tone.

"Why were you parked there?" Raynes asks when Sean finally stops to take a breath. He stares at the ground. Now, this is a move I recognize. Sean hesitates, perhaps unsure how much to disclose or whether to lie outright.

He appears to pick door number one. "We bowl on Tuesday nights at the Elmsdale Lanes. We have a few beers, so someone is the designated driver each week. When it's Lou's turn to drive, I park my car in the CCC lot and leave it there overnight. Lou drives me home, and my dad drops me off in the morning to pick up my truck."

Somehow Raynes has got a notebook in his hand, and he is pushing it across to Sean. "Give me the name of the league, who plays on the team, and Lou's contact info." Sean reaches for the notebook and writes. In a few minutes, we're back at our cars. The stars are still out. It isn't even 6:30.

As if reading my thoughts, Raynes says, "Let's grab a bite to eat. I won't tell Tiffany if you want to go to Timmys."

In Nova Scotia, Tim Hortons is the go-to spot for coffee, donuts, muffins, and more. Regulars meet up there to start their day or grab a bite of lunch. The wait staff calls you "honey" and "dear." Tiffany would be beside herself to think I'm eating there. I tell Raynes to count me in.

Because Timmys, as everyone calls the North American chain, is so popular in Nova Scotia, it's not unusual to find one on every corner or thereabouts. The nearest one from us is less than five minutes away. Raynes has two coffees on order when I walk through the door. "What would you like?"

Since I have no idea what Timmys serves for breakfast, I tell him to surprise me. He brings me two breakfast sandwiches, one on a biscuit with sausage, the other on a bagel with bacon. It may be one of the best breakfasts I've eaten in years.

Raynes grins. "I take it you like Timmys?"

"I do now," I say, grinning.

"What did you think of Gillis's story?"

This may be a test or a request for confirmation of his assessment. Or both. "Sounded like he was telling the truth. It also explains why the truck would reappear in the lot. Surely, if you were the murderer, you wouldn't come back to the scene of the crime so colourfully."

"I'm thinking the same thing, although I'm not supposed to tell you that since you are not officially a police officer, even if you did earn a merit badge this morning." Raynes pauses, then continues. "We'll confirm his alibi, but it's too detailed to be fictional. I'll also check with Faye Bedwell to see if she or Norm knew this fellow, but I doubt it. And make no doubt; this murder was personal."

I hadn't thought about that. Why would someone want Norm dead, innocuous Norman Bedwell? "How do you know it's personal?"

"The crime scene." Raynes says this as if it answers my question. It doesn't. He takes a breath and looks at me. "We're eliminating outside suspects."

That sounds good to me. The shorter the list, the less work it takes to identify the real killer. If the outsiders are getting crossed off, it's likely an insider. "Shit."

"You might want to prepare yourself. It well could hit the fan."

So much for enjoying breakfast.

* * *

Marcia is waiting for me when I arrive at the office. She is pristine in a charcoal grey long-sleeve mock dress with matching shoes. She has a list and passes it to me without elaboration: recommended auditors. Of course, it is.

"Zahra Bashir also called." I wonder why Bashir didn't call me herself. She has my number. Marcia reads my mind. "She tried your cell but didn't get an answer."

Now I have two calls to make: auditor and CCN, but I have to call Thorne and Susan Warrington first. I start with my HR director. Susan is in my office within minutes. She's wearing a slate pantsuit with a muted silver blouse that hugs the lapels of her blazer. I'm assuming the lack of color in the attire this morning has to do with showing respect for the recently deceased. I'm glad I opted for a basic black blazer and white shirt.

"What's up?" Susan sounds a little wary. She reaches for a file on my desk and absently straightens it.

I explain about the auditor and the need for three quotes. Susan visibly relaxes. We're all on edge with Norm's death hanging over us. I must make a point of doing a walk-

165

around through the plant and the admin office. I've read being visible and accessible is important.

"Have you reached out to Faye?"

"I have. She's grateful we continue to show how much we cared for Norm."

I swear Susan's eyebrow went up. What is it around here with eyebrows? I must check what that means. "I think we should begin the hunt for Norm's replacement. I don't want it to seem callous, but we need a CFO. Have you talked to Faye about this?"

I have. "All good on that front. We can put a timeline in place for the new hire." Susan nods, straightens another file on my desk, and heads for the door.

My next call is to Thorne, who picks up on the first ring. "I was wondering when I'd hear from you. Bashir is recycling her news. She must be chomping at the bit."

"It appears so. She called this morning."

Thorne recommends staying clear of her, and he thinks we have the perfect out: compassion. "Let her know our priority is to support the police investigation, and out of respect for the family, we have nothing further to say at this time. She'll push you for more but keep repeating that."

Part of me wonders if I should run this by the senator, but I'm ignoring that part of me. I dial Bashir's cell, hoping the reporter is mid-interview somewhere and unavailable. She answers on the first ring and foregoes any preamble. "We'd like to do a follow-up with you. Are you available later this morning?"

"Our first priority is to support the police investigation, and out of respect for the family, we have nothing further to say at this time," I tell her.

"Nothing we talk about will impede the investigation," she counters.

"Out of respect for the family, we have nothing further to say at this time," I repeat.

"You'd think the family would want to hear from you, to know you care enough to speak out about this issue." Bashir is pushing a button.

She misdials on this one. "Our first priority is to support the police investigation, and out of respect for the family, we have nothing further to say at this time." I repeat my key message once more.

"What will you do if the murderer is someone from CCC?" Bashir ignores my well-crafted mantra.

"Will you be disappointed if it isn't?" I snap back. So, she did push the right button after all. "Our first priority is to support the police investigation, and out of respect for the family, we have nothing further to say at this time." I hang up.

* * *

In hindsight, I'm pleased with the way the non-interview went. There's nothing

Bashir can use against us, even my little retort. For my snappish reply to make sense, the reporter must include her question, and I'm guessing she doesn't want to do that. At least not now, anyway. That leaves Bashir with only me staying on message. I don't know what she will do with my "no thanks" response to her interview request in the long term, but she is a responsible journalist. She might nudge me or make a jab, but she will not create a fictitious rewriting of our conversation.

I also have to give the seasoned reporter credit for knowing what will likely get a rise or an unintended response. Bashir did make one comment that is sticking with me: Norm's family needs to know we care. While I think we've done that, the doing has been more personal than public. I have an idea of how we could change that, but I need a barometer by which to gauge its merit.

Tiffany answers the phone on the first ring. "Everything okay?"

I sense her concern. I don't usually call home during the day. "I have an idea I want to run by you." I can feel her beaming along 20 kilometres of fibre optic cable. "I was thinking CCC should officially name its boardroom the Norm Bedwell Meeting Room or something like that. We could have a small ceremony with some food. Faye and Bran could come and cut a ribbon or something. I've already mentioned this to Faye."

I swear my wife is crying. I can hear the catch in her throat. "That's perfect. I can help if you'd like."

"Let me run it by Susan and Michael to make sure there are no HR or legal issues, and we can chat about it tonight. I appreciate your help."

Since my day seems to have meandered once more along the Norm Bedwell Murder Trail, I give in with little effort to return to the work on my desk. I call Susan and Michael, who pop by my office without complaint. Norm's death is taking a toll on productivity in the C-suite.

Neither director has direct or significant concerns about the idea. Neither also knows I've already mentioned it to Faye and Tiffany. Susan thinks it would send an important message to staff, show we care, and all that. She says it might also help to bring closure, and Michael agrees, although he does raise an interesting point about precedence. The next time someone dies, do we have to name a room after them? We all agree the circumstances surrounding Norm's death are atypical enough that we will treat this as a unique situation for now.

"There is another consideration," Michael says, just as I think we're about to wrap up. "What if the killer is someone who works at CCC?"

Susan is appalled. Or perhaps that's outrage. Or defensiveness. I have to spend more time learning to distinguish emotion. I must subscribe to TikTok. "Why would you ever think that?" There is heat in the asking.

"It's not that far-fetched," I point out. "One of our budmasters is under suspicion for theft at the moment."

"That's a far cry from murder," Susan says. I'm pretty sure that was defensiveness.

"What if it is an inside job?" I deflect the conversation and turn to Michael. I realize I'm beginning to sound like a *Law & Order* rerun.

"If we honor Norm this way, the room will also become synonymous with the fact that a colleague killed him," Michael says in response to my question.

"Good point." We debate the pros and cons of the room for a few more minutes and land back where we started. There are more advantages to naming the boardroom after Norm, and we decide to hold the ceremony in a week. That will give us time to get a plaque, arrange catering, and reach out to staff to attend. I've been tasked with inviting Faye and Bran. I'll also be running the inside murderer issue by Tiffany tonight to see what she thinks.

* * *

I don't know if it's the call earlier today or a moment of weakness, but Tiffany has cooked real food for supper. We're having burgers, hamburgers, with her mother's hashbrown casserole, or so I'm informed when I comment on how great something smells. I'm also told we'll have company. And right on cue, Raynes rings the front doorbell.

"Thank you for including me." He looks at Tiffany and hands me a bottle of Nova 7, an aromatic white wine that is a favorite of my wife's and many other Nova Scotians. For me, there is a bag from The Grind. It's a pound of Koa from Hawaii. I'm impressed. "The clerk recommended it." It would appear I'm easy to please. I should work on that.

I have no idea what prompted the dinner invitation. I don't think Raynes is either, but it doesn't matter. "Glad you're here," I say quietly and somewhat conspiratorially. "We're having actual meat. It's a big deal."

Tiffany can sense we're uncertain why we are called together or what is significant enough to warrant actual beef. She holds off until the burgers and hashbrowns are in front of us. There's also kale salad, but I'm not touching that. Neither is Raynes.

"I thought it would be nice for the three of us to share a meal," Tiffany says. We're not buying that, and she knows it. "I also thought it would be nice for Lin to hear about the plans for the boardroom." Tiffany looks at me. Raynes follows suit.

I have no idea what is going on. I'm sure it shows. I take a few seconds and count to five. "We decided today that CCC would name its boardroom in Norm's honor. Have a bit of a ceremony. Invite the family and staff. Have a few munchies."

"Isn't that wonderful?" Tiffany asks. And now I see it. Raynes and I are expected to bond because I'm a nice guy. Raynes sees it, too, I'm sure, but seems distracted. He reaches for the kale salad before realizing what he is doing.

"There is one potential issue that came up today." I mention this to get past the moment and onto a more comfortable ground. "Michael wondered about the implications if the murderer is a CCC employee?"

Tiffany is appalled. Or outraged. Or defensive. Dammit, I have to figure out the difference between those three. "That would never happen."

"That the killer is someone in my company, or the boardroom name might be sullied?"

"Either. Both," Tiffany says quickly and firmly.

I look at Raynes. He has drifted for a minute, until our gazes bring him back. "Truth is killers usually work close to home. There is a good possibility that whoever did this is an employee, a supplier, or a courier. Someone with easy access to CCC and its offices."

Tiffany's shoulders slump. Tonight was supposed to be a celebration, the continued development of a truly special bromance.

Raynes can sense her disappointment. "That said, I think the honor would outweigh any criminal outcome. And it would certainly mean a lot to the family."

My wife perks up. It was the right thing to say for both of us. The ceremony is back on, and I'm quite pleased with myself and the day.

"I was wondering if I could attend the ceremony." Now, it's Raynes who's a little uncertain. "Quietly and unobtrusively."

The beam is back on Tiffany's face. She doesn't care why Raynes wants to spend time in my vicinity, just that he does. I, however, do care.

Without waiting for me to ask why, Raynes explains his request. "If the murderer is with CCC, they'll likely attend the event. It might help me to watch people's reactions and speak respectfully with a few of them about Norm."

It makes sense. I nod. "Good idea. I'd like this to be over."

Raynes nods. Tiffany does not.

After supper – Tiffany carries out a cheesecake from Costco with real processed sugar and canned cherries –

Raynes and I settle in the den with a cup of the Koa he brought. I see the expression on his face.

"God, this is good." Raynes grins.

I laugh.

"I have some good news and some bad news for you." Raynes turns solemn. I brace. "Clay Brandt confessed to theft."

I'm disappointed but not shocked. The budmaster's criminal activity will be a bone of contention with the senator and the regulator. Or maybe not.

"Confessed is not quite accurate," says Raynes. "He cut a deal."

"What did he have to deal with?" I ask, a little taken aback. The crime was small time by everyone's account.

"It seems the cannabis Brandt was taking from CCC was supplementing a much larger cannabis business. He's part of it and gave up the grower and distributor. We shut down a grow op with 11,000 plants this morning."

"Good god." I am genuinely startled. "That's huge. We have roughly the same number, and you know how many square feet we require."

"That's the beauty of rural Nova Scotia. Lots of farm country to set up an outdoor and indoor operation."

"So, this is big." There is a sigh in my voice.

"Here's where the good news comes in. Brandt will serve two years less a day. That means no federal prison. It also means no trial, no publicity, no media."

As far as I'm concerned, Tiffany can invite Lin Raynes to dinner whenever she wants.

* * *

It's 10 a.m., and I'm standing in Norm Bedwell's office for some reason I can't fathom. On my way to the lunchroom for a coffee refill, I unexpectedly end up here. Something nags at me, and I don't know what. But I believe it's in this room.

Pondering is not my style; fixing things is. That said, I like to get things right, and there is something not right about this room. It's been bothering me since Raynes said he knew Norm's death was murder because of the crime scene.

The room is much like it was on the day of Norm's death. This sets me back. I assumed Susan would have arranged for its dismantling once the police finished, yet nothing appears to have changed. Several items are missing, however. The yellow police tape is gone, of course. The thick beige rope hanging from the ceiling was removed along with Norm's laptop.

The mahogany desk with its pockmarks and pits holds center stage. The large beige and green rug continues to consume much of the office. The stain, Norm's bodily fluid, remains visible. The dogs continue to play poker. The stacks of paper are curling slightly, reminding me to ask Susan if they've been reviewed, should be distributed, or destroyed.

One of the two black-webbed chairs remains in front of the mahogany table as if awaiting a visitor. The other is in the middle of Norm's office and strikes me as unusual. Then I remember the rope hanging from a metal beam in the ceiling. During design, this seemed like a good feature, contemporary and, frankly, a way to save on drywall and paint. I am rethinking that decision now. The lone black chair is like an exclamation mark in the emptiness of the room. Not too long ago, a noose literally hung above it.

I walk around the office as if inspiration will strike, answers will fall into place, and my life magically will revert back in time. There's no eureka moment, however, just me, some dusty furniture, a large stain, and a lone exclamation mark.

I find myself back in my office, calling Faye Bedwell, not realizing I know her phone number without looking it up and no idea why I'm dialing it. She answers on the second ring. I recall getting tasked with formally inviting her to the boardroom event next week. Normally, I would have drafted something to say, or at the very least, bullet points. I do not like winging things. And yet, here I am, flying without a net. "I wanted to check in to see how you and Bran are doing," I say.

I can tell she is pleased. "We're coping. Things are much easier now that the bullying situation is resolved."

"Is it?" I do not want to sound disbelieving, but in my experience, a bully is a bully.

"For now." Faye shares my opinion of bullies.

"I have another reason for calling, and please feel no obligation to say 'yes.'" I can sense Faye's anticipation and hesitation. "As I mentioned earlier, the team at CCC would like to rename our boardroom after Norm, and we're having a small ceremony next Wednesday afternoon. We wondered if you and Bran would like to come."

I hear her sniffles, and now she's in tears. Dammit.

I should have anticipated this. It's what happens when people are moved, and this is the kind of shit that moves them. I know this means I've done a good job and hit a responsive nerve, but tears are not my forte. I should have made this call with Tiffany. Between tears, Faye thanks me and accepts the invitation. I offer to pick her up – what the fuck is wrong with me today! – and she says that would be wonderful. I also tell her if she would like to say a few words, that would be welcome, but I recognize it may be too difficult. Faye asks for time to think about this, and I promise to send her details about the event via email. We end the call a few seconds later.

It occurs to me that this renaming of the boardroom is, in fact, becoming an event. We've been calling it that, for lack of a better word. Turns out, it's the right word. It has to go without a hitch. I ask Marcia to send a request to the senior management team. Within a few minutes, we have a meeting time set for tomorrow morning. Then, in keeping with the lack of control that has mysteriously and resentfully defined my day, I invite Tiffany to the meeting. She's as gobsmacked as I am.

"You know Faye and her son better than anyone else who will be in that room. I want this to go well for them."

Now she's in tears. Dammit.

Chapter 9

It's been a difficult day. In fact, it's been a helluva week. I can't wait to get home, get a drink, and get some control back in my life. I pack up a few files, fully intending to do some work tonight in the stillness and quiet of my home office. Maybe I'll crack open a green-tipped bourbon arabica coffee from St. Helena. I have been saving it for a special occasion. Getting my life back falls in this category.

I should know better than to assume things will go as planned.

Tiffany has the door open before I even turn the knob. She's wearing a white cami with spaghetti straps, nicely contrasting with her darker skin. What she's not wearing is a bra. Her nipples are hard, pushing against the silk.

Dammit. Tiffany is horny.

I like sex, don't get me wrong. I like sex with Tiffany. She's warm and wet, sexy and receptive. She moans softly. What I don't like is having to wait, or work, for her to come. And I don't like the damn cuddling that always follows. It's like some idiot wrote a rule book for women.

But there is no getting away from it. Along with the seductive top and sloppy smile is a glass of wine. My guess is it's not the first. Sure enough, Tiffany offers me a drink from a half-empty bottle of Nova 7 as she reaches for my crotch and slurs ever so slightly, "Fuck me."

And like that, I'm hard.

My wife is well-lubricated in every sense of the word. She arches her back and wraps her legs around me before I have a chance to take her in my mouth. The moans are not so soft now. I'm harder, and I'm ready. So is Tiffany it appears. I know this because Tiffany drapes her arms around my chest as I roll out and off her. Now we cuddle. I sigh and begin my meditation mantra.

* * *

As I shower the next morning, I wonder how Tiffany will handle the day. Hungover may not be the best attire for her first CCC staff meeting. Wrong again. By the time I'm dried, dressed, and heading into the kitchen for my first cup of coffee, Tiffany already has fruit on the table and a Columbian dark roast waiting in the French press. She's downright breezy, with good reason.

My wife shines without claiming the spotlight. I'm a spotlight kind of guy.

I get a hug, a kiss, and a smile. I tense, anticipating tears, but the moment passes, and we are on the schedule for the day. It's all about the upcoming meeting. Tiffany can't wait, although she tries to rein in her enthusiasm. I worry I've made a mistake inviting her, but that's what happens when you don't have bullet points.

Tiffany and I travel separately. She'll arrive closer to the 10 a.m. meeting time. I will have a few hours to sit at my desk and finish some work. Miraculously, everything goes according to plan.

We start the senior staff meeting off innocently enough, talking about food and the notice to employees. Managers will ensure staff is on the third floor at least 10 minutes before the beginning remarks. It's clear we want a full house.

I let everyone know I've contacted Faye and invited her and Bran to join us. There's some shuffling. I don't know if this is disagreement or discomfort. I make a mental note to ask Tiffany later. At Raynes's request, I don't let them know he'll be attending.

Susan Warrington drops the first piece of bad news into the agenda. The plaque will not be ready for next week, at least not the plaque she and I selected. Tiffany suggests we get an artist's rendering or visual of the plaque that can be unveiled instead. We can clarify it takes time for quality and are prepared to wait. Maybe my wife should attend all my staff meetings.

The task falls to Susan, as have most of the arrangements. Tiffany offers to help with logistics, and Susan shoots me a glance for confirmation. Sure, why not? What could go wrong?

We make the decision that I will speak as CEO. My remarks will be on behalf of the company. Quietly and almost deferentially, as if not wanting to speak out of turn, Tiffany asks if it would be a good idea to invite Norm's assistant, Charlene Smith, to say a few words personally. If she's up for it.

By now, the management team is as impressed with my wife as I am. We agree it's a good idea, and Susan will ask Charlene if she'd like to do this. No pressure.

Then comes the difficult discussion we've been skirting around since the naming of the boardroom after Norm first arose. We don't want to seem cavalier or callous. We also don't want to be maudlin. How do we frame this now-increasingly celebratory event given the context?

We're embedded in a circular discussion of the optics when Tiffany says softly, "Perhaps the focus could be on Norm's life, his contribution, his family. We could say, truthfully, that we have come together to honor the man and acknowledge his contribution to us in this small way."

Well, fuck me.

* * *

The day continues to go well. I call the senator to update him on all things CCC, a weekly check-in. He's in a good mood and asks not only how Tiffany is doing, but how things are going with me. It's not our usual conversation starter.

When I mention the boardroom-naming event, he hesitates. "Riel, that's a great idea. Good thinking."

My father-in-law is not one for praise, high or faint. I smile. Things are finally going my way. That sense of optimism, fleeting I'll soon learn, may explain why I reach for the phone and ask Susan Warrington to come to my office. Something continues to nag at me about Norm's office, and evidently, I'm unwilling to let it go.

The HR director, as usual, is prompt. At times, I wonder if there are secret hidden channels I don't know about that let people arrive at my door within minutes of being summoned. Susan, permed hair in place, green tweed suit pressed, jade earrings setting off the outfit flawlessly, takes a seat in front of my desk. She's relaxed and unhurried.

"What are the plans for Norm's office?"

Not a question Susan is expecting. "What do you mean?"

"Are we clearing out furniture? Repainting?" There is a slight edge to my voice. I wonder if I'm deliberately ruffling a feather.

"Well, the police are through and have given us the go-ahead to get back to normal," Susan stumbles over the last word as if difficult for her.

"I'd like to leave the room as it is for a little while longer." I offer no explanation for this unusual request.

Good try, but Susan doesn't let that go. "Why?" She remains relaxed and unhurried.

It's a shrewd question, and I do not have an intelligent response. "I don't know," I answer honestly. "It just seems like the right thing to do for now."

The ambiguity of my response seems to satisfy Susan, but it raises another important question. "What will we do with the office during the naming ceremony? We don't want Faye and Bran to see it," she says.

The third-floor executive area, as I like to think of it, is a rectangle. Offices are positioned along the outer walls to allow for a window view. The internal space comprises the kitchen area, boardroom, and meeting space. Norm's office is to the left of the entryway and the path closest to the boardroom.

"We'll take the long way around. Let's put up some signage directing people to the right, and we'll keep someone on the door to ensure nobody heads in the wrong direction, meaning Faye or Bran."

Susan suggests putting a welcome table at the entrance to the offices that will help to partially block access to Norm's side of the floor. We'll have a simple sign with Norm's name and "Boardroom Ceremony" written on it and a flower bouquet. "This will be an appropriate entry point. I don't think anyone will connect this to wanting to keep people from Norm's office," Susan says.

I agree. There's another smile from Susan. This is going to go well.

* * *

In hindsight, I should have braced myself for the unexpected. That's what happens in a crowd of people when emotions run high. It's boardroom ceremony day. The sun is out; it doesn't give off any heat, but that is typical November in Nova Scotia. The fall foliage flutters on the trees, and the sun glints through a canvas of reds, greens, and yellows. An upbeat energy permeates throughout the building as if we have something to celebrate. The thermostat is higher than usual, double digits. (I'll let you do the conversion).

The day starts smoothly enough. Tiffany and I pick up Faye and Bran (who appears very formal in his grey suit and periwinkle blue tie). He shakes my hand and thanks me. I see Tiffany tear up out of the corner of my eye. So, this is an emotional moment.

I take advantage of it, kneel on one leg, and place a hand on Bran's shoulder. "We all loved your dad. You're very much like him."

Now both Tiffany and Faye have tears running down their faces. I put an arm around Bran's shoulders and stand up. I am getting good at this.

When we reach the office, Tiffany guides the Bedwells smoothly to the right and directly to the boardroom. She's been briefed on the danger of heading left. The boardroom looks excellent. It is respectfully celebratory. There are fresh flowers in a vase and an easel with the artist's rendering of the plaque, currently covered. Bran will unveil it. This was Tiffany's idea. We ran it by Faye, who ran it by Bran.

The room is filling up. As usual, the managers have come through. There is one unexpected guest, though, at least from their perspective. Raynes arrives about 20 minutes early. He goes over to Faye and Bran and gives the former a quick hug and the latter a handshake. Then he heads my way.

"This is nice." He nods at the décor and the crowd.

"I hope it also turns out nicely for you." Raynes knows what I'm talking about, exactly.

"I do have an update for you. Sean Gillis's alibi checks out. He was bowling that night. Friends drove him home and picked him up the next morning."

This is not news; Gillis was a long shot. But we're running out of suspects. Raynes raises his left eyebrow, possibly conveying the same conclusion.

At 2 p.m. on the dot, Susan gives me the signal to start. Thorne has written remarks that are short, straightforward, and moving. I sound sincere. I look at the employees, at Faye and Bran. I hold my gaze. It's textbook. Then I turn the podium over to Charlene Smith, Norm's executive assistant. She is 12 seconds into her remarks when she breaks down. Tiffany moves forward to bolster her, and somehow Charlene makes it through the next four harrowing minutes. Then it's back to me. Susan and Tiffany have choreographed the event almost down to the second. I should have expected a misstep. God, plans, and all that.

It's time for the unveiling. I let everyone know that we've arranged for a special plaque to honor and celebrate Norm Bedwell's life, and I ask Bran to step forward and unveil the artist's rendering for us. With all the solemnity of his 11 years, Bran moves forward slowly. He stares at the floor. Tiffany jerks her head almost imperceptibly in my direction.

I'm not quite sure why, but I move in his direction. "I'd be honored to help." Bran nods, head down. We're at the easel. He reaches out and flips the cloth covering back. He stares at the image of his father on the left of the board. It's a casual rendering of Norm at the office, wearing a cream-colored crewneck sweater and leaning back in his well-worn chair. He's smiling. I realize Norm appears happy in this picture. The words The Norm Bedwell Boardroom are on the right of the artist's rendering.

I step to the side as this is Bran's moment. He turns around and looks at everyone. I can see pride. Then it's confusion, like a deer caught in the headlights. I'm sure people will think it is sweet.

Suddenly there is a grey and blue blur, and it is coming directly at me. I have no idea what is happening, but I feel the impact of 85 pounds hitting me mid-center. I manage to stay upright as Bran Bedwell wraps his arms around my waist, his face rams against my stomach. Between tears, he says, "I love you."

There's nothing for it. I'm back down on one knee, "I love you, too." The room is completely silent for three interminable seconds. I'm not certain if I've done the right thing. At the fourth second, the room erupts in applause. Bran looks up, startled and pleased. I must remember to send the video to the senator.

The crowd is mingling now and munching on danishes in Norm's honor.

People awkwardly approach Faye and Bran to offer condolences and share a few memories. Some of the staff moved toward me, thanking me for doing this. I'm can't fathom why the event seems to hold such importance, but I am well read on the issue of building trust and connections. I realize that's what we've done here today.

Within 20 minutes, the crowd thins. Faye steps over to thank me and asks if it's okay if they leave now. They both have had an emotional day. I get ready to escort them out when Tiffany says she'll drive them home, and I can finish up here.

"We don't want to take up any more of your time," says Faye, sounding appreciative.

"Please, any time you need anything, call."

The tears are back in her eyes. I don't know why, but I ask if she and Bran might like the artist's rendering. Now the tears spill over. Bran marches resolutely to the easel and removes the foam core board. Without looking at anyone directly, he heads for the door.

Somehow it has been decided, Raynes will drive me home and stay for supper. It turns out that's a good thing. Tiffany will pick up pizza. Real pizza.

* * *

There is a rhythm to dinner á la Raynes. The three of us gather in the kitchen, sip our beverage of choice (wine, wine, beer), and sit down to eat. The suppertime conversation is easy, flows smoothly, and consumes minutes effortlessly. Post-dessert, Raynes and I exit the kitchen and chat over coffee, usually in my home office. That's when we get down to business, although I'm not always sure what that business is until Raynes tells me.

Tonight, as it turns out, there's not much business. Raynes gives me more detail on Mr. Orange Truck. His parents account for his early-morning hours. At 32, he still lives at home. The GPS confirms no mileage is unaccounted for and, most importantly, no link can be found between the young lumberyard bowler and Norm Bedwell. Their lifestyles, ages, professions, and even neighbourhoods are different, and no threads, however remote, connect them.

"What does that mean for the investigation?"

"It's good news and bad news." On the plus side, Raynes informs me, one more suspect has been eliminated. On the downside, we're running out of suspects.

"More and more it appears like this had to be someone with access to CCC. At the very least, someone who knew Norm well enough for him to take them to his office." Raynes doesn't meet my eyes. There seems to be something mesmerizing about his coffee.

The detective doesn't need to spell out the implications of an in-house murder for me. Regulators will be all over us. I take a sip of the Brazilian Mogiana Raynes brought as a thank-you for dinner. "You're getting good at this." I nod toward my cup.

"And you're getting good at the detective work." Raynes is not laughing, and his left eyebrow remains firmly in place.

"Not from any desire for a new career," I say honestly, but with a bit of a grin. "I did do something strange, though. Maybe you are rubbing off."

Raynes tilts his head. Curious. "I went back to Norm's office to look around. Something's off, but I can't quite put my finger on what it is."

"You will."

Now I'm curious. "You know what's out of place?"

"I know what caught my eye when I first saw the scene."

"And you're not going to tell me." It's not a question.

"I'm hoping when you identify what is out of place, it will hit you who most likely would connect to this type of anomaly."

"How much time do we have to resolve this?"

"We're coming up on three weeks now. The investigation will slow down as we eliminate suspects and find fewer clues. It will always be an open case, but it will start to get cold within the next few weeks."

That timeline aligns with mine. I can't keep Bedwell's office on lockdown forever. At some point, we'll have a new comptroller. Life will go on.

"Did you glean anything from the boardroom event today?" I ask this, but I already know the answer. If there were something to be found, Raynes would have told me long before now. The telling, I have come to understand, is not because we are friends, whatever that means, but because I am a conduit to information and insight that could prove useful in finding a killer. It's a new role for me. But then again, so is the role of friend.

"I'm ruling out people. More by gut than evidence in some cases, mind you."

"What do you mean?"

"Well, I spoke with everyone there today. Made a point of it. It's clear, aside from managers in the plant, employees in production didn't know Norm. Some didn't even know who he was before the murder. Hard to imagine they'd have a reason to kill a stranger. They don't even have a reason to be on that side of the building."

"What about the managers?"

"Same thing. While they knew Bedwell, contact was limited. People don't usually kill randomly. No one has a reason to murder Norm Bedwell as far as I can determine."

"Then it must be someone in the inner circle." It's more to myself than to Raynes.

The HPD detective nods. "It's likely. And those are people you know well."

"I can't believe you didn't consider me a suspect." I'm smiling.

"Oh, I did," Raynes says, also smiling. "Your alibi checked out. A neighbour saw you take out the compost bin and leave the house about 45 minutes later. That ruled out being at the office committing murder."

It had never occurred to me I might be a suspect, and thanks to a witness I didn't know existed until now, my innocence has been proven. Had to be Mrs. Dunlevy. Nosy neighbour. God bless her.

* * *

It's Thursday morning, and I slept well but briefly. My conversation with Raynes keeps repeating itself. I've learned to listen to those voices in my head, especially when they intrude on my morning meditation. I grab the yogurt/granola/fruit concoction Tiffany has stocked in the fridge, gulp down a coffee (which I am usually loathe to do), and jump in the car.

I'm back in the office. To be precise, I'm back in Norm Bedwell's office, trying to soak up the ambiance in hopes a clue will magically present itself. It doesn't. Indeed, nothing happens except for me standing in the middle of a dead man's office waiting for inspiration.

I start going through my executive team alphabetically hoping that the sign I'm searching for will reveal itself as I review what I know about each of them. Evidently, I have time to waste.

I have six senior managers who report directly to me, and five are still alive.

Delroy Brown is the director of operations. He grew up in Jamaica and in the cannabis industry. That hands-on skill drew him to a land that boasts snow and ice, at least for part of the year. The truth is, we ardently recruited Delroy. He's knowledgeable without being arrogant and willing to try new methods of production and new plant strains. He also smokes the stuff ardently. His experience, as PR people say, is lived.

As far as I can tell, Delroy's team respects the 6' 3' Black man with bulging biceps and a gentle patois. The management team also likes him and respects the work he does, which is innovative and excellent. I've not known him and Norm to clash; that said, operations is always angling for more money, and the comptroller is always attempting to reduce spending. I mean, who kills over a few thousand dollars earmarked for their job? On the personal side, I can't imagine Norm and Delroy in a bromance. Delroy is happily single and playing whatever field he can; Norm seemed rooted to his family and dog painting.

The same disconnect appears evident, at least to me, with Lucy Chen, our chief compliance officer, although she and Norm appear to share more common ground. Lucy's background is in banking. She likes numbers. I assume she'd like Norm for that reason and vice versa. Lucy is buttoned up and careful. Her white blouses are always perfectly pressed, and she thinks before she speaks. We all rely on her to tell us when we are potentially stepping outside a regulation, rule, bylaw, or other constraints. Norm would have done the same, although with a little less chilliness.

I think back to staff meetings. It seems to me Lucy and Norm were usually aligned in their thinking. After all, they're both risk-averse by profession and perhaps personality. I don't remember any contrived closeness, secret smiles, or shared absences from the office. But then again, would I?

Like Norm and Lucy, our chief legal counsel, Michael Graves, is risk averse, a quality that may align well with a senior position in the cannabis sector. Customers can be wild, free, and unabashedly cool. We cannot. Michael has earned the high regard of the management team, and that's somewhat of a coup. The Dalhousie University law grad is young, early thirties, and this is his first solo-at-the-helm job. He's acing it. He's also one of the few people who spent time with Norm. As I reflect on times when Norm and I intersected, I can see him having lunch with Michael in the staff kitchen. Whether this was planned or happenstance, I don't know, but they liked each other's company. Perhaps it's a parenthood thing.

There might be a personal motive for murder buried somewhere in Michael's relationship with Norm, but I couldn't come up with it.

Nor could I see any reasons why Neela Khoury, our IT director, or Susan Warrington, our HR director, would want Norm dead. Susan interacted with Norm more than Neela, maybe more than any of us, but that was the nature of her job. Neela sparred with Norm more than most, but then she sparred with most of us. Neela believes non-techies don't understand her profession or its supreme importance. She's probably right.

As I emerge from my reverie, ready to leave Norm's office, I realize I'm not alone. Marcia is standing a few feet away, perfectly pressed in a cream pantsuit with a teal scarf, patiently waiting for me to come down to earth. "You're meeting about the auditor is starting now," she says. "I put a Green Mountain light roast on your desk."

This woman is a human divining rod.

Susan and Michael are waiting for me when I walk into my office. They are impatient to dive in. We start with an update on the hiring process and quickly wander off in numerous other paths, most of them relevant. As my two senior managers simultaneously inform me about auditor choices and the possible legal implications of whatever that person finds, Marcia knocks on my door and enters without being invited.

She doesn't wait for a query from me and says, "Tiffany called. She would like you to call her right away. She says nothing is wrong, but she needs to tell you something that is timely."

Susan and Michael gather their laptops and assorted papers. It's like the White House has called on the red phone. Michael plucks his left eyebrow, and I assume that means he's concerned.

"Can you give me 15 minutes and then we'll resume?" I ask, but we all know it's not a question.

I'm reaching for the phone before everyone is out the door. Tiffany is not an alarmist and knows how to contain and constrain herself. If she's interrupting a meeting, it's important.

Tiffany answers on the first ring. "Sorry to interrupt your day, but Faye Bedwell called me, and I wanted to give you a head's up."

So now I know the context. Innocuous enough, I think. I'm wrong.

"Next Wednesday Bran's class is going to the Discovery Centre. The school asked for volunteer chaperones. Faye is wondering if you would volunteer and go with Bran. She knows you're busy, but Bran is floundering without his father, and he has taken to you."

Silence descends. Several profane words run through my mind, but that's an involuntary response. I don't like being caught off guard or lack of control. As I breathe more deeply, in and out, those thoughts shift. What is the right response?

Tiffany answers as if she heard my inner dialogue, "I think you should go, if you can. It would be nice for Bran, and Faye. It would also send an important message to staff, regulators, and others about you and the industry."

Well, fuck me. I'm going to a science center – with kids.

Chapter 10

I'm on edge about the Bran thing. Interacting with children does not come naturally to me, and I don't like situations that force me outside my comfort zone. I'm used to short interactions where charm, nods, and expressions that mirror sincerity are all that's needed. Longer excursions in unfamiliar environments pluck my nerve. It's when I turn to yoga, meditation, and an Italian dark roast.

I spent the next few days and most of the weekend getting back to normal. My normal.

Tiffany senses something is up, and she's overly solicitous. For her that means making something vegan, like it is a treat we can both indulge in. The highlight of the weekend is a teriyaki tofu bowl. Usually, it's the equivalent of mulch.

I'm feeling more like myself and more productive by Monday morning. The outside auditor tops my to-do list. I meet with Lucy, Susan, and Michael, and we decide on whom to hire: a highly recommended woman who runs her own consulting firm. She's experienced, affordable, and not deterred by the presence of purple kush. She also got the thumb's up from Lucy, therefore got my vote, and will start work by Wednesday, when I'm off having the time of my life with 40 kids at the Discovery Centre.

My good mood lasts until lunch when Raynes calls. "There is someone I'd like you to meet," he says. "Are you free this afternoon?"

The seasoned police detective makes this sound like a friendly invitation to connect with his favorite buddy. I know better. "What's up?"

"We have your hate-mail writer coming in for an interview. I was hoping you could watch from behind the one-way and let me know when anything is amiss." Raynes delivers this message as if discussing a weekly poker game.

I don't know how to say "no" or if I should. "What time would you like me there?"

"Four o'clock," Raynes says. There is the slightest hesitation. "Why don't you bring Tiffany? We can have dinner at my place and discuss what we've heard. The evening traffic will be over by the time we've finished."

Of course, Tiffany is thrilled. She wonders if she should bring something. I suggest she shop while I'm at the Halifax police station – swanky Spring Garden Road is nearby – and pick something up there. At the very least, dessert will be made with real butter and flour.

I let Marcia know I'll be out for much of the afternoon and unavailable. She nods conspiratorially. I can't wait for Norm's killer to be caught.

The drive from Elmsdale to Halifax takes about 35 minutes. It's a straight line down the 102 that at some point becomes the 118, although it is unclear why the number changes. The sun's out, there is little traffic since most people are at work, and no roadwork slows us down. The fall foliage gives its last hurrah, and I find myself enjoying the moment for no reason. It's a pleasant day, and I don't have to juggle any crises for half an hour.

Tiffany is downright effervescent on the drive into the city. She burbles on about what a delightful break this is from the daily grind, how kind of Raynes to include her, what his house will be like, and if he can cook. The continuous conversation is welcome. I retreat into my thoughts and prepare for the upcoming interview.

It's 3:20 when I drop Tiffany at the top of Spring Garden, the busiest street east of Sainte-Catherine in Montreal. She seems to be looking forward to spending time in Halifax and spending money. I'm glad for her. She deserves this afternoon's delight.

The police station is only minutes away in downtown Halifax, and there is ample parking. I'm walking toward the main doors of the station when Raynes walks out. It's like he has ESP. "I thought you might be early. Gives us time to talk first."

Instead of heading back into the station, Raynes turns right toward Gottingen Street. This predominantly Black neighborhood was once the heart of Halifax's shopping district and is now revitalizing itself. "We'll grab a coffee at Seven Bays," Raynes offers by way of explanation.

I soon find out the café is also a bouldering center, where people chart a path and climb in the name of physical fitness. Unlike a climbing gym, the "boulders" are moved so climbers can chart a new course with each visit. There is also no need for harnesses or ropes.

I'm intrigued. "It's fun," says Raynes, sensing my interest in the activity. "We should come sometime."

Now, I don't know how to interpret this, so I sidestep. "Let's catch Norm's killer first."

"Maybe we'll have some luck this afternoon." Raynes doesn't sound hopeful.

We grab two Costa Rican medium roasts and head back toward the station. As we're walking, Raynes fills me in. The man getting interviewed is Logan Kendall, 56, white, and very angry about the legalization of cannabis. His son died addicted to crystal meth, a drug Logan believes he got hooked on because he started smoking weed. The contention that marijuana is a gateway drug is one of the arguments put forward to stop legalization. It's a contention I don't think has merit, and one the industry has spent millions debunking.

Raynes must have read my dismissal of Kendall's belief. "You don't think he's right?"

"Not from what I've read." One look at Raynes's face tells me he disagrees. I try the eyebrow thing and fail.

"Two years in narcotics, and I never met a tweaker who didn't smoke weed," Raynes says, looking down.

"Bet your tweakers also drank alcohol," I respond calmly. "Want to reduce addiction – including drug addiction – make booze illegal."

"Good god, no," says Raynes, and he laughs as he opens the double-glass doors to the police station.

The interrogation rooms are on the second floor, and we're in the third and final room on the left. Raynes settles me in behind the one-way mirror. He's wearing an earpiece, so I'm to let him know if there are any questions I think he should ask or if anything Kendall says isn't accurate. A young man in a black constable's uniform is in the room to ensure all the tech is working, the session is recorded, and I can transmit info to Raynes if necessary.

About three minutes later, another constable leads Logan Kendall into the interrogation room. Logan's about 5'11" and at least 60 pounds overweight, wearing blue jeans and a Black Sabbath t-shirt. He doesn't appear nervous. In fact, the reverse, like he's almost itching for a fight. We wait 10 minutes for Raynes to show up, a strategy, I'm sure.

"My apologies," the detective says as he settles himself into a chair across from Kendall. "Boss needed an update."

If that was supposed to make Kendall worried, it didn't. The Black Sabbath t-shirt leans in and says sarcastically, "Hope it went well."

Raynes pivots. "You're in a lot of trouble, Logan. Charges are pending."

The threat seems to roll off Kendall like water off a duck. Maybe he doesn't care if he is in trouble with the police or if he doesn't believe he is. I doubt I could be as cool as he appears. But in keeping with his air of bravado, he puts both hands on the grey plastic table in front of him, slides forward only inches from Raynes's nose, and says, "Well, charge me then."

"My pleasure," says Raynes, who gets up and calmly leaves the room. A smile hovers at the corner of his mouth.

A minute later, he glides through the door to the viewing room where the technician and I are sitting in somewhat stunned silence, settles comfortably into a chair next to me, and sums up the interview with one word. "Arsehole."

"What now?" I ask.

"Now we decide whether to charge him," Raynes says as if this was obvious.

"Do we have enough?" I say wondering when the correct pronoun became "we."

"That is up to you."

He goes on to explain that Logan Kendall has, without a doubt, sent the threatening emails identified by CCC as the most egregious. The IP address used to send the emails was easily unveiled and traced directly back to Kendall. Apparently, the middle-aged plumber is not a world-class cyber whiz.

"We know he did this, and we also know uttering threats is a crime. The question is," says Raynes, "does CCC want to see this man prosecuted?"

I'm a little shocked it's up to me. "I thought the police laid charges in criminal cases?"

"We do," Raynes explains, "but depending on the nature of the crime, we often determine if those affected want to bother with a criminal charge, trial, and possible publicity."

And there it is. The real reason I'm here. The dilemma is whether CCC wants to be the big bad company that smacks down a grieving parent. "What would you recommend?" I ask Raynes.

"A lateral arabesque." The detective can sense my confusion. "My sister studied ballet for years."

I'm still confused.

Raynes lays it out for me. "Let's sidestep the question for now. I have another idea to get us where we want to go."

"I have an idea I'm not going to like this." I'm a fast learner.

"What if we put you in the room with Kendall and see what falls out," Raynes says. I can't tell if he's smiling.

"What if we don't," I reply, hoping my sarcasm is evident.

In the end, as usual, Raynes wins out. Two minutes later the door to the interrogation room swings open, and I walk in with the detective. "Charges are up to this man," says Raynes by way of succinct explanation. "I'll be back in 10 minutes."

I move to the only other chair in the room and extend my hand as I sit down. It was not a fitting gesture.

Kendall swipes it aside and says, not nicely, "I know who you are."

"Good," I reply. "That will save us time." I don't like arseholes, either.

"There is nothing you have to say that I care about," Kendall sneers.

"Sir, my job is to protect my employees and my family. You jeopardized both." I stop to see if this has made any impact. It hasn't.

"Poor baby," Kendall says. The sneer may be permanently etched on his face. There is not a bead of sweat anywhere.

I know how to squash a human being like a bug, and Raynes gave me a few additional ideas in the five feet from the viewing room to the interrogation room. I go for the jugular. "I didn't realize you don't care about protecting the people you are responsible for, the people you love."

And suddenly, there he is, the raging man. Kendall is on his feet. Veins pulse; fists clench. "Don't you tell me I didn't love my son. I did everything I could to save his life. You people and your easy drugs killed him."

"We didn't kill anybody," I say, attempting to diffuse the anger. My tone is calm. "You didn't kill anybody. Addiction did."

"How do you think he got addicted?" Kendall snaps. "You made it too easy to get drugs."

"No one made it easy to get crystal meth," I point out reasonably. "Your government legalized cannabis, but there is an ocean of difference between weed and meth. That difference is addiction."

"Save it," Kendall snaps. "I've heard it all before."

"You should find out what you're talking about," I say, with a slight edge. "Facts are very helpful things, I've found."

"Fuck you," says Kendall.

Now, I'm annoyed and must be careful not to lose control. I do a three-part breath, hold for three, exhale for three. More calmly, I turn to Kendall and tilt my head. "You're not a stupid man."

That seems to take him aback. "Fuck you," he says. Perhaps I am wrong.

"You've been spouting your venom for months and months. This is the first time anyone has cared enough to find out who you are and bring you in for questioning. Why do you think that is?"

"You're too busy getting kids hooked on weed," Kendall snaps back.

"Think again." I lean in. "Think hard."

At last, Black Sabbath t-shirt seems to cotton on to the fact that this may be about more than a few fetid emails. "What are you talking about?"

"Murder."

"What the fuck. I didn't murder anybody."

"Well, you better start talking and fast," I say. "Because I have a dead colleague, and there is a cop out there who will stop at nothing to find out why. And whom."

On cue, Raynes enters. Kendall is on his feet, shouting objections and innocence. Raynes shuts him up with a single look. And just like that, it's all over. The bravado is gone. In its place, a man slumps over a table, burdened by the pain of a son who died too young and much too pointlessly.

Kendall has no alibi, but Raynes knew that going in, or at least suspected it. What he wants, and what Kendall willingly gives him, is access to his computer and his cell phone. It will help determine where Black Sabbath was and when. And, at least for now, it puts the issue of charges on the back burner.

As we're about to leave the room, Raynes turns to Kendall and says, gently, "Just so you know, Norm Bedwell went to church every Sunday and never smoked weed in his life."

Kendall looks up. "Who the fuck is Norm Bedwell?"

* * *

In the 10 minutes it takes us to get to the car and navigate the evening traffic to pick up Tiffany, Raynes and I discuss and dismiss Logan Kendall as a possible killer. We agree he doesn't have the expertise to enter a secure facility like CCC, and he definitely doesn't know who Norm Bedwell is. Another suspect bites the dust.

"You can push us to press charges," Raynes notes. "He did break the law."

"I can't see any advantage to charging this man, and I can see several disadvantages," I say. "I don't want to be the cannabis CEO who tries to crush a grieving father. But let me check with Michael and

Lucy to see if we need to consider any legal or compliance issues."

Tiffany is waiting for us when we pull up to the corner of Spring Garden Road and Dresden Row, although it took us a minute to identify her underneath all the shopping bags. "I had such a great afternoon," she says breathlessly.

"We can tell," I respond with a grin.

Raynes lives in the North End, a predominantly Black community in the city. His house is about 20 minutes away in rush hour, such as it is in Halifax. Agricola Street is a residential, commercial, historical, and contemporary mix. The once blue-collar neighborhood is slowly changing. It's becoming upscale and upmarket.

Raynes's house is up near Lady Hammond Road. Grassy medians divide the street, and many homes lining each side date back more than a century. Raynes's is one of those.

It's exactly what I expected, and yet totally unexpected. The wood exterior is painted a slate grey (expected), and the trim is a deep aquamarine (unexpected).

Tiffany's graphic design senses are pleased. "It's lovely," she says, and undoubtedly means it.

"You sound surprised." Raynes smiles.

"A little," she admits, "but mostly, you live like you look."

The 6'4" detective doubles over with laughter. Glad he and my wife are having such a good time. There is some snark in that thought until I realize the sentiment is sincere.

Inside the 126-year-old house, the color scheme is white (expected) with various vivid trims (lavender, ochre, teal, all unexpected). The design is minimalist (expected); the atmosphere is cozy (unexpected).

"Dinner is all ready. I just have to heat a few things," says Raynes. "Riel, would you grab some wine from the fridge?"

Inside the brushed chrome Whirlpool refrigerator sits two bottles of Nova 7, so we know the meal is catered toward Tiffany. Raynes directs me to glasses, and I pour a drink for my wife. Before I can pour one for myself, Raynes silently points me to a Shiraz sitting on the counter. I can feel myself smile.

Raynes tells us to make ourselves at home, but there's no need. Tiffany has her shoes off, showing the other clotheshorse in the room each of her purchases. The clothing gets the seal of approval.

I'm fine with being excluded. This evening, indeed the entire day, will make Tiffany happy. It's something she doesn't get a lot of here. Her family and friends from childhood and university live in another country. She works as a graphic designer from home with clients, primarily political and mainly in the U.S. She deserves this.

Raynes bustles around, and soon a delicious aroma fills the kitchen. He catches my disbelief and curiosity. "We're having seafood chowder. It's an old family recipe. It's not vegan, but it's healthy – well, a little healthy. And there is a secret ingredient."

Dinner is, in fact, delicious. Tiffany and I have second servings of the chowder plump with haddock, shrimp, scallops, and lobster. Homemade biscuits, warm from the oven, accompany the meal.

"These are divine," Tiffany says. "Did you make them?"

The implication is clear – he didn't – but not offensive. "My Mom baked them fresh for us," says Raynes. "She keeps me well stocked."

"I didn't realize your mother lived here," I say without thinking. I mean, why would I know anything about his parents?

"My mom and dad are both here. Only a few streets over," Raynes says. "I'm hoping you'll meet them one day."

I'm so shocked I take my focus off the food. Raynes doesn't miss a micro-expression. "Well, I want you to meet my dad. I've told him you are restoring a 1968 Camaro."

I have no idea how Raynes knows about the Camaro. The car was a project of mine before we landed in Nova Scotia four years ago. It's a weekend retreat for me and a bit of a passion. My dad and I have restored cars together since I wore diapers. Mind you, I wasn't much help at that stage. As I learned to walk and talk, I contributed much more. Now, I have my restoration project in a country my father has yet to visit. I don't talk much about the Camaro, my progress, or my plans. (It's all about suspension at the moment.)

Raynes's inside info about what lies inside my garage must have come via Tiffany, but it doesn't matter. It's dinner chitchat, and I'm very good at the superficial. "If your mother bakes me biscuits, your dad will be the first to drive in the car when it's ready for the road," I say. I may even mean it.

I'm reaching for my third biscuit, made with flour, salt, and a sprinkle of heaven, when Raynes alerts me to save room for a completely different biscuit. The final course of the meal is blueberry grunt, a traditional Nova Scotia dessert that faintly resembles a cobbler, but gets prepared on the stovetop.

"It's said," Raynes tells us as we dive in, "that you can hear the blueberries grunt as the steam rises from the biscuits."

"I don't know about the blueberries, but I can hear my husband grunting with delight," says Tiffany, and everyone laughs. It's funny and also true.

The meal is delicious, the discussion light and topical, and the evening pleasant. Raynes serves up coffee, both delectable and new to me. "You've perked my interest in coffee, pun intended. It's a Guatemalan bean from Dope Coffee in Atlanta. I thought you'd enjoy the flavour – organic, of course," he says, glancing at Tiffany, "and the company name."

We're almost ready to leave when Raynes brings us back to one last piece of murderous business. "Since you helped get the Baillies to cooperate, I wanted to let you know we've cleared the family. The GPS tracks."

"I thought the mileage was off," I say, confused.

"It was and we found out why." The detective looks at Tiffany and me to see if we deduce why the mileage is not what was reported.

And one of us can. "The kid drove the car without the parents' permission," says Tiffany matter of factly.

Now that had never occurred to me, but it makes perfect sense. I see Tiffany with renewed respect. "I did it all the time when I was young," she says.

Who the hell is this woman?

* * *

We're at the door, saying goodbye and thank you. I'm almost to the car when Raynes calls me back. He has a bag of biscuits and a container of chowder for me.

"Tiffany aced you as a detective," he says with a smile, "but you did get one over on her."

My confusion shows.

"Want to know the secret ingredient in the chowder?" Raynes asks.

I'm mid-nod when he leans in and says with a grin, "Salt pork."

Chapter 11

Wednesday arrives much more quickly than I'd hoped. I have no signs of the flu or any other communicable disease, and the Discovery Centre did not burn down in the middle of the night. There are no excuses to extricate myself from the school field trip. Tiffany is effusive about what a great day we'll have, how wonderful this is for Bran, and how nice of me to go. She's definitely worried. I share her concern.

I'm not a father. I'm not an empath. My personal prefix before "path" precludes that. For the brief time I knew my biological father, he was an asshole. I know from reading my huge file from Santa Barbara Child Protective Services, not because I remember the man or have had contact with him for the last 35 years. Mateo and Elena Brava adopted me as I was turning three. They raised, loved, and supported me, and they continue to do so. Unfortunately, what the damaged asshole did in the first two years of my life was permanent.

But today, I have to act fatherly. At least uncle-y. Tiffany has been giving me tips all week while pretending not to give me tips. "I wonder what Bran likes to do in his spare time. I must ask him that the next time I see him." OR "I remember being 11. I certainly did not like to hold hands with any adult." OR "I always want to act cool with kids, but they see right through me. I need to learn it's better just to be myself."

Bran is waiting on the curb when I arrive to pick him up. I know we're going to gather at the school and go by bus to the museum. I don't why I couldn't have met the kid in the school parking lot, but Tiffany's face made it crystal clear the idea was a terrible one.

I pull into the curb, and Bran is halfway into the front seat before I've even come to a complete stop. "Thank you," he says. For what? I haven't the faintest idea.

"This will be fun." I'm lying.

Faye is waving from the front step. Bran and I both wave back. "So, tell me what we get to do today?" It's the first of a list of questions I've prepared.

From what I know, most kids are monosyllabic. The expected answer to my question, so I read, is "Dunno." (Hence the need for a list.) Bran is not like most kids. "We teach a robot how to walk through a maze. And we solve some cube thing using animation. And we make music with another cube. And we get to play with touch tables. Do you know what they are?" Bran inhales a much-needed breath.

I admit touch tables are not on my list of prepared questions, so I avoid it. "Sounds like a fun day." To my surprise, I mean it.

The school parking lot is awash with cars, kids, teachers, and other adults. There's general chaos. Only the driver seems relaxed, leaning against the big yellow bus, playing some game on his phone. Bran grabs my hand – so much for Tiffany's tips – and leads me to a woman with a clipboard, standing in the eye of the storm. Bran tells me this is his teacher, Ms. LeBlanc. She's wearing a pink sweater draped neatly but casually over blue pants and appears in control and comfortable.

"Thanks for doing this," she says. "We'll be leaving in about 10 minutes."

Bran grabs my hand again and leads me to the bus. "Let's sit up front. You can see more from there."

Maybe because I'm with Bran or because he is exceptionally excited, the bus driver nods his approval, and we walk up the three steel steps. Bran runs over to the second row and claims the seat by the window. "The teachers sit in the first row," he says by way of explanation for his choice.

I'm mentally bringing up my list of questions, but there is no need. Bran is too excited. He hasn't been to the Discovery Centre since he was a kid, I'm told, and begins a recitation of all the wonders of the place. I learn it's four storeys high with more than 40,000 square feet of space. "And it's the newest science museum in the country," Bran says at breakneck speed.

His soliloquy is interrupted by the first of the kids and their adjacent adults entering the bus. Before we get under way, Ms. LeBlanc gives us instructions for when we land: no wandering away, no yelling, no punching, no touching anything that says, "Do not touch." While on the bus, speak quietly. I assume we are allowed to breathe.

Now we're on the highway to Halifax, and the volume in the bus has reached a fever pitch. I'm unsure if this is excitement or normal chatter for boys and girls. Bran is saying something to me, but I can't hear a word out of the kid's mouth. I catch Ms. LeBlanc's eye. She smiles and shrugs. So much for instructions.

We're outside the Discovery Centre in downtown Halifax with 91 over-active tweens. The adults are slowly separating themselves from the pre-adolescent throng like algae from a right whale. I can't move anywhere; Bran is clenching my hand so tightly I may be losing circulation. I'm learning the key to a field trip is to take a head count every 22 minutes.

Ms. LeBlanc nods. All the kids are accounted for. "Let's go," she says, and there is a mass movement forward, much like water running through a funnel. Bran is dragging me now. For the next three hours we climb inside a giant Rubik's Cube, make our way via robot through a maze, and animate the bejesus out of ourselves. I had the time of my life.

"That was fun," I say as we head to the bus.

Bran seems a little dejected.

"Didn't you like it?"

"No, it was great," he says. But I don't believe him.

In cases like this, I do what I always do, call Tiffany. I instruct Bran, "You go get our lunch." I nod toward the bus. "I'll meet you back here. I have to go to the washroom."

Bran heads toward the yellow bus, and I step around the corner.

Tiffany answers on the first ring, "Everything okay?"

"I thought so, but Bran seems sad."

"That's good. It means he doesn't want the day to end."

Dammit. I should have known that. "Thanks," I say. I mean it.

We're all taking our box lunches to the Whale Tail sculpture on the Halifax waterfront. It's a colossal carving that serves as a slide for kids. While the adults eat quietly, the kids romp, run, and slide their asses off in this last breath of freedom. I don't know where they get the energy.

I'm glad for the break, from Bran, from concentrating, and from trying to figure out how to build a robot. I retreat into my ham and cheese on whole wheat when I realize I'm under scrutiny. All the other volunteer chaperones are women. It appears I'm an anomaly and apparently an attractive one. One look I do know: when I'm being given the once-over.

I'm 6'1", athletic, with dark black hair, and black eyes. I walk with confidence, and I take time with my appearance. Today it's khaki chinos with a short-sleeve burgundy crewneck. I do look good. I smile at the ladies and scan the crowd for Bran. He's already making his way back to me.

"Want to stake out our territory on the bus?" I ask. He beams.

The ride back is much different from the one we took to the Discovery Centre. The kids are quiet, well quieter. The adults are deflated, and relieved. Everyone seems subdued. Conversation, if it happens at all, is muted. Some of the kids and one adult are asleep.

Bran, also subdued, asks if I had a good time. I assure him I did. "Thank you for asking me."

"My dad almost always used to come," he says. "He'd take off work, and we'd spend the whole day together."

"Your dad loved you very much."

"I know." Bran's head is bowed. "I just wish he could have come on our last trip, but he was away with you for that company thing in Toronto."

I'm sure kids get things wrong, but to be honest, Bran doesn't strike me as that kind of kid. I never went on an overnight trip with Norm, and we have no company affiliations in Toronto. "I'm trying to remember," I say. I'm not sure if I'm deflecting or probing. Please Lord, let it be the former.

Bran wants to talk. I don't know if it's about bonding with me or unloading about his dad, but in the 35-minute drive back to the school parking lot, I learned all was not right with the Bedwell household in the months leading up to Norm's death.

We're interrupted by Ms. LeBlanc, who goes through the rules on getting off the bus and home. I take this opportunity to text Raynes. "Meet Bran and me at Scoops. 30 minutes."

I don't know what the fuck is wrong with me.

* * *

Scoops is the hot spot in Enfield if you want ice cream and other cold confectionaries. As we're leaving the bus, I ask Bran if he'd like to go for a sundae. I assume when he flings his arms around my waist, that means "yes." I'm grappling with how to tell him about Raynes.

Raynes saves me the trouble. By the time we arrive, the detective is already standing outside Scoops. He glances at me quickly and forms one word silently: Tiffany. He places his hand on Bran's shoulder and says, "So, the first text I get from this guy says, 'I'm inside a freakin' Rubik's Cube.' The second one shouts, 'I'm building a robot.' The last one: 'Best day ever.'"

Bran's smile extends beyond his ears. The grip on my hand tightens.

"Riel said you were coming here, and I wondered if I could crash?"

Bran nods, the smile etched on his face.

By the time we sit down – three hot fudge sundaes with a dash of caramel sauce, sprinkles, and marshmallows – Raynes has us feeling like the three musketeers, one for all and all for one. I make them promise not to tell Tiffany what I'm eating, and everyone laughs.

Raynes leads us gently and expertly where he wants us to go. He looks at Bran. "You had quite the day."

We both nod, and Bran reviews the highlights of everything we saw and did.

Raynes lets him run with it, laughing and showing interest in every word. When Bran pauses for a mouthful of vanilla ice cream submerged in sauce, Raynes says quietly, but naturally, "I remember field trips with my dad. Did you get to go on field trips with yours?"

Bran nods, a little downcast. I interject, hoping to sound remorseful. "I may have botched the last one. Norm came with me to Toronto for a company meeting." Over Bran's head, I signal Raynes: No.

Bran comes to my rescue. "It wasn't your fault. Dad had to work. We all understood that, especially the last six months with the new acquisition."

Bright as Bran may be, I don't think he knows what an acquisition is. He has heard this term somewhere, and the somewhere is Norm.

Raynes looks at me and raises his left eyebrow ever so slightly. He knows as well as I do that there is no acquisition and never was.

"It's a very busy time in the company," I say, largely to fill the space.

"I missed him most at night," Bran says, mostly to himself. "He always read me a story when I went to bed. Mom tries, but it isn't the same."

"He told me how much he missed doing that," I say, convincing myself it's in the cause of uncovering more info but dreading that maybe it's because I like the kid.

"Dad said you made it as nice at the office for working late as possible, and there was even a place to sleep when people had to work late." Bran is settling back in the role of storyteller and reciter of facts.

There is, of course, no place for people to sleep at the office, and frankly, no one works that late. It's obvious something had been up with Norm, and the something was likely someone. Faye isn't an idiot. How did Norm get this past her?

"Sounds like your dad made the best of a bad situation," Raynes says.

"Well, he liked the job and the people he worked with." Bran glances at me. "He liked his assistant a lot. She's great."

Well, who knew? Norm, you dog you.

The conversation shifts back to the Discovery Centre and robots. A half-hour later, we're saying goodbye to Scoops and heading for our cars. Bran and I wave to Raynes. He says quietly, "I'll see you shortly. Tiffany invited me to dinner."

Of course, she did. The man may as well move in. Then again, maybe we'll have real food.

* * *

I'm starting to like it when Raynes comes for supper. Tonight, we have meatloaf, mashed potatoes, and brussels sprouts with bacon. The butter on the potatoes and the bacon aren't likely real, but they're a close second. There's no doubt, however, that the meatloaf is real. There's even something called tuxedo cake for dessert. She must have purchased it from Costco or M&M, but who cares? The cake has actual chocolate in it. I have two servings.

I sense Tiffany's disapproval as I extend my plate for the second helping. She tries not to frown or sigh and fails on both counts.

Raynes picks up easily on her displeasure. "And this is on top of a chocolate fudge sundae with extra caramel sauce," he says with a laugh. I shoot him a look, and he laughs louder. For some reason, Tiffany is smiling.

As usual, my wife disappears as the coffee comes out. It's a dark roast Italian billed as pesticide free, bird friendly, and shade grown. Worth every pigeon that ever swooped down for a nibble. I'm relaxed, full, and content, like the coffee. I should know better by now.

"I have a favour to ask," Raynes says, and once again, I do not like it when the HPD detective comes to supper.

"Of course, you do," I say out loud and realize it is too late.

Raynes laughs. "I'd like to interview Bedwell's assistant."

"You don't need me for that," I answer. Being sated evidently slows you down.

"In your office, with you there," Raynes says, completing his sentence.

Now I'm sitting upright. "Why?"

"We interviewed everyone of likely interest following Bedwell's death. That included his assistant, Charlene Smith," Raynes says en route to an explanation. "We're always searching for two things: incrimination and information. We eliminated Smith as a suspect, then. But that doesn't mean she doesn't have more information to offer. Especially now that we have a better sense of what we need from her."

"Smith is gay," Raynes says in answer to my unasked question.

"So unlikely to have had a torrid affair with her male boss."

"Unlikely," Raynes agrees. The smile is back. "But I bet she knows her boss, his habits, and his behaviour better than almost anyone. If we can make her feel fairly comfortable, she may recall something or share something she'd be otherwise reluctant to tell us."

"And you think she'd be comfortable in my office?" I ask this with a hint of incredulity. "I am the CEO."

"Well, it's your place or mine – an office or an interrogation room at the Halifax police station."

"My office it is."

* * *

I drop by Charlene's office first thing Thursday morning. She's a woman who is both punctual and organized. Her brushed maple desk is clear of knickknacks, budget files are neatly stacked by year, and a lone coffee cup sits within easy reach and arm's length away from her keyboard. Charlene is a little dazed to see me. I concentrate on sounding casual and ask if I might have a few minutes of her time around 10 o'clock. The casual fails to work its charm. I see the fear on Charlene's face. I assure her the meeting is nothing to worry about.

So much for my assurances. I'm barely back in my office when Susan Warrington breaches the door. She hasn't even buttoned her navy-blue blazer. "Why do you want to see Charlene Smith?"

I don't like my HR director's tone, but I am curious about the source of her knowledge. "Just a few things to discuss," I say without saying anything.

"If there are any HR issues, I should be in the room," Susan says. "Charlene called me. She's concerned."

"There are no HR issues," I assure her. I understand I'm being petulant, but I like being petulant. And I'm CEO. I can be petulant if I want.

Susan is fussing with a pen holder on my desk, aligning it parallel with the edge of the desk frame. "Well, let me know if there is anything I can do."

I give in. Susan has good ideas, and she cares about the company. "Lin Raynes wants to ask her a few questions, and he thought she'd be more comfortable here than at the police station."

"What in heaven's name could he want with Charlene?"

"Beats me," I say. Petulantly.

* * *

Charlene arrives promptly at 10 a.m. Marcia ushers her in like a mother hen rounding up a lost chick. The chick is about 5'6" and 140ish pounds. She has short brown hair and eyes to match. Most people would describe the 28-year-old as "average" and in no need of clucking.

I smile and motion for Charlene to sit on the sofa to the left of my desk. Raynes is already seated in an adjacent chair. I can see the shock written all over Charlene's face.

"Detective Raynes is hoping you might be able to provide more insight into Norm the man," I explain. "You're not obligated to answer any questions if you don't want." I lean in and smile. I am getting good at this stuff.

"I'm fine," Charlene says. She isn't. I can see why Charlene picked up the phone to call Susan Warrington the instant I exited her office. She's nervous as hell and repeatedly follows the pleat line of her tartan skirt with thumb and forefinger, back and forth, back and forth. Apparently, everyone in this company has some sort of tic. I should play poker with them.

"I'm going to get right to the point." Raynes leans in. I wonder if he got that from me. I'm also wondering if the bluntness is for his benefit or Charlene's. "We've learned Mr. Bedwell may have been having an affair. We're hoping you might know."

Charlene hesitates. She doesn't gasp or move to instant denial. Does that mean the answer to Raynes's question is "yes"?

Nope. "I don't know." Charlene lifts her eyes for the first time.

Raynes waits.

Charlene moves to fill the silence, as expected. "The last few months, six maybe, Norm was often in the office after I left. That wasn't normal. Usually, he rushed out the door at five to be home for supper and to help Bran with his school projects." Charlene pauses.

Raynes continues to wait patiently. Without moving a muscle, he manages to convey encouragement. I must learn to do that.

"I offered to stay late, but Norm always said he was finishing up or getting ready for a meeting the next day. But I kept his schedule and most times, there was no meeting. So, no need for his preparation."

At last, the silent police detective speaks. "And you thought something was wrong?"

"It just wasn't normal," Charlene says. "I like normal, and so does Norm. So did Norm. It's one of the reasons we got along so well."

"Did you have any reason to think there were problems for Norm at home?" Raynes asks.

"Everything seemed good on the home front," Charlene says. "He talked with Faye the usual number of times, and Bran called every day right after he got home from school. Norm loved those calls."

"Yet you think something was off." Raynes pushes gently.

Charlene turns to me for confirmation.

"It's fine. You're being very helpful," I assure her.

"It was the dentist's appointments," says Charlene by way of non-explanation. "He had a lot of dentist appointments all of a sudden, and they never stopped. There could be two or three a week."

I'm attempting to align dentist appointments with late nights and a torrid, okay, semi-torrid affair. I'm coming up blank. Raynes isn't. "You think there were no appointments, at least not with the dentist?"

"I did wonder," says Charlene. "He also seemed happier, at least at first. You know that glow of love and everything. I even heard him giggle on the phone once."

"What do you mean 'at first'?" Raynes asks.

It's a good question, and I missed it.

"The last month, Norm was out of sorts. He seemed distracted, which was not like him at all. And he was fretting about something. I told myself it was probably the bullying problem with Bran."

"You think the affair was ending," Raynes says.

"If it was, Norm was the one doing the ending," says Charlene. She has our attention. "Norm was starting to go home at the regular time, buy flowers for Faye and toys for Bran. He was acting like his old self. And he cancelled several dentist appointments."

"You know Norm, perhaps as well as anyone," says Raynes, pausing. Charlene and I are poised for what comes next. "Do you have any idea who Norm could have been sleeping with?"

Charlene stares at the floor.

I'm on tenterhooks.

"No," she says, "I honestly don't. And I've given this a lot of thought."

Again, I thank Charlene and tell her how helpful she's been. Raynes asks if she will keep this conversation to herself.

Charlene nods and leaves the room. I hear her exhale, finally, as she walks out of my office.

"Was that helpful?" I ask Raynes once we're alone.

"It was. We know two things we didn't before and can assume a few others. First, I learned Norm's behaviour was different the last six months of his life. It's likely an affair and certainly easy enough to confirm the dentist appointments."

"It may be in our open calendar system." I quickly see that it means nothing to Raynes. "When we schedule meetings, we can see everyone's calendar to check their availability. Work-related appointments are visible, but personal time is blocked off. We don't know why someone isn't available to meet, but we know they are not."

"Who would see the blocked time?"

"Anyone who has access to his computer."

"Charlene and maybe Faye," Raynes says, primarily to himself.

"What else did we learn?" I prompt, using the plural pronoun because he never gave the second thing he learned.

He's about to answer when Marcia walks in with two Caffè Americanos and a lemon loaf from Starbucks.

"Good god, yes," I say to her. "Don't ever leave me."

Marcia doesn't bat an eyelash. Before we can exhale, the coffee and loaf are on the table in front of the sofa. So are cream, sugar, and napkins.

Raynes is impressed. "Is she always like that?"

"Without fail. I'm convinced she's enchanted."

"If anything ever happens to you, she'll know who did it," Raynes says with a laugh.

"No," I counter, "she'll warn me in advance."

I learn from Raynes that we've learned Norm was having an affair (probably), and it lasted about six months until it apparently came to, or was coming to, an end. On the assumption side: the person is likely someone Norm saw regularly. And by that, Raynes means someone who works for CCC.

"We combed through Bedwell's cell phone. There were no texts, deleted or otherwise," Raynes says. "So, how do you make arrangements with your lover?"

You make them over the office phone or by talking to them in the building.

Dammit.

* * *

Raynes looks like he's getting ready to leave. Looks can be deceiving. He lingers for a second. "Have you ever had a donair?"

Donairs are a Halifax specialty. Some residents contend this is Nova Scotia's official food. Aficionados spend a great deal of time discussing the nuances of the dish, thin slices of spiced beef on a warm pita, sprinkled with diced onion and tomato, and swimming in a sweet, garlicky sauce. Or so I've been told. To answer Raynes's question, "No, I've never had a donair."

"Let's go." He pauses for a split second. "I won't tell Tiffany."

I'm in. We head to the Donair Queen in Elmsdale, a play, I assume, on the King of Donair in Halifax, where the dish is said to have originated.

I let Raynes order for me. "Two donairs," he says.

Apparently, it's not complicated.

The decor is fast food meets comfort food. You order cafeteria-style and either head out or grab a seat. Most people do the former. A few plastic chairs and tables are scattered at the back of the restaurant. Raynes and I stake out a table in the corner. Only one other person is eating inside.

For the next 15 minutes, Raynes and I concentrate on demolishing our donair. It's not as easy as it sounds. The meat, toppings, and sauce are rammed into a loosely folded pita and blanketed with a small piece of tinfoil. No matter where you bite, something falls out or spills over from another place. I see why Raynes grabbed a large handful of napkins.

"What do you think?" Raynes asks when we've finally swallowed the last sloppy morsel.

"I think I'm in heaven. Let's do this every week. And if Tiffany finds out, my marriage will be over."

Raynes laughs.

It feels casual and natural. And I should know better. "You want something, don't you?"

The detective laughs again but has the decency to be embarrassed this time. "No, and yes."

The favour is not small and, in hindsight, not unexpected. Raynes needs to talk with Faye about the affair to see what she may know and what she may not know she knows. He'd like me to be there. To be more accurate, Raynes anticipates that Faye will want me there. He believes she'll be more relaxed and open if I'm there.

There is, it seems, no time like the present. While my system digests slow-cooked spicy beef, Raynes reaches out to Faye. She agrees and asks if I could be there. Faye seems to sense, or Raynes somehow implies, this will not be an easy conversation. He suggests we meet at her house if she can leave work. She can. I notice we're meeting before school gets out.

Faye gives me a hug when we arrive. I don't know if this is because she's Nova Scotian, she wants an ally, or she thinks we're friends. I made a mental note to ask Tiffany. Faye has put tea on, Morses, the favorite local blend, and sets out a tray of homemade chocolate chip cookies.

I take a seat on the couch. Faye sits beside me. Raynes pulls up a chair and sits directly in front of us, separated only by the coffee table. He takes a sip of tea and a bite of cookie. He puts both down and looks at Faye. "I hate to do this, but I have some questions for you that will not be easy."

"You think Norm has done something wrong, don't you?" Faye is almost breathless. She reaches for my hand.

"I don't know," says Raynes, "but I'm hoping you can help me figure it out. Did you recently notice any strange or different behaviour from your husband?"

"You've asked me this before." Faye sits a little taller, stiffer. "My answer hasn't changed." She's defensive. I must ask Raynes why.

"We've learned Norm was working late and even spent some nights at the office or away on business trips." Raynes's tone is neutral, even calming.

"He's been very busy this last quarter, even earlier, but that's because of the acquisition," Faye says.

"There was no acquisition." Raynes's tone is less neutral and less calming.

"What do you mean? Of course, there's an acquisition." Faye sounds both indignant and confused. I wonder if you can be both. Faye stares at me. "Tell him." Now that's indignant.

I look at her gently. "There's no acquisition. There was never an acquisition." I reach for her hand, mirroring her earlier gesture.

"What do you mean? Of course, there's an acquisition." Faye's face moves from me to Raynes and back again. Neither of us says a word. We wait. "Are you telling me there was never any fucking acquisition?"

Faye will have to grapple with that reality and what it meant for the last several months of her marriage.

But Raynes doesn't have time to wait for that reflection. He pushes forward. "There is some indication Norm may have been having an affair." His tone is back in neutral.

"With a woman?" Faye's voice has risen.

"We were hoping you could tell us," Raynes says.

Suddenly Faye is deflated. Her shoulders slump; the indignation is gone. "Is it someone I know?"

"We don't know," Raynes says, repeating his mantra. "We were hoping you could tell us."

Faye seems nonplussed at the suggestion. "The only women I've ever heard Norm talk about are his colleagues. Neela. Susan. Lucy. Charlene."

She is facing me now. "Are you saying one of these women screwed my husband and then killed him?"

"The detective is just trying to understand what was going on in Norm's life before he died," I say, speaking for the first time. It appears I did a good job.

Faye turns her mind to her suspect list. "Well, Charlene is out. You know why?" she asks, looking first at me, then at Raynes.

"We do," says Raynes. I must admit I admired Faye at that moment. Despite the fact we had turned her life upside down she protects a friend. Faye wasn't going to be the one to out her. That's loyalty.

"Neela's out," says Faye. "She's a practising Muslim. Norm is a practising Christian. That's like oil and water.

"It can't be Susan. She's too ambitious. Even if you have thwarted that ambition by claiming the CEO spot." Faye is facing me now. I see the hint of a smile.

"Susan will not do anything to jeopardize her climb to the top. Besides, her parents are older, and she spends most of her free time helping them. She's a good person."

"So that leaves Lucy," says Raynes quietly.

Faye laughs. "Wouldn't that be ironic? Your ethics officer has none." She seems to savour the irony for a moment. "But it's not Lucy. Norm didn't like Lucy."

"How do you know?" Raynes asks. He almost sounds like background noise.

"We have a rule over supper. You have to talk about your day, good and bad. We keep it simple for Bran. But when he leaves to do his homework, we always continue, diving a little deeper. You know, adult stuff.

"Norm thought Lucy was a fraud. He said she didn't give a damn about doing the right thing, this was just a job for her. To Norm, rules were everything. Accounting is built on rules.”

“But Norm broke the rules,” Raynes points out. It’s almost a whisper.

“Norm broke our rules. He always held himself and everyone else accountable for doing their job without blemish. He thought Lucy was blemished.”

“Did he always feel that way?” I ask. I’m wondering if this was a cover Norm used. It’s a tactic I’ve used in the past, pretend you don’t like something or someone that you really do.

“From the start,” says Faye. “In the very first staff meeting, Lucy said her job was to point out compliance requirements and make sure staff were informed. Norm was disgusted. He said she didn’t even know her job was making people toe the line.”

* * *

I imagine Faye is glad to see us leave. Raynes agrees. “What do you think?”

“I have no idea what to think. Faye didn’t know Norm was having an affair, yet she had a list of suspects. Then she eliminated each one of them. Is that unusual?”

“In my experience, most affairs are with someone known to each spouse, so Faye’s list is not likely wrong. What’s wrong is her analysis. One of those women is probably

240

our murderer. We just have to figure out which one.”

As it turned out, we'd have it figured out by morning.

Chapter 12

It's now 3:30 and no point in going back to the office. Raynes and I stop at Cup of Soul in Elmsdale and get three lattes and three cinnamon buns. Then we head back to my place.

Tiffany wasn't expecting this but is delighted to see us. We're forgiven for bearing treats with processed sugar.

It takes Raynes all of 62 seconds to blurt out, "Riel ate a donair."

Tiffany is mortified.

So am I. "What happened to the code of silence?" My outrage is not feigned.

"My allegiance is to Tiffany," Raynes says. "Always." And like that, all is right with the world. If this man were American, he would be my running mate for vice president.

"Riel has been helping me again. Do you mind if I steal him for a few more minutes?"

She doesn't mind at all, of course. Tiffany also reminds me she has her book club this evening. It's a neighborhood group, mostly women, wine, and gluten-free grub.

I'm glad to see her get out and even more glad she has never asked me to join.

"You're on your own for dinner." She looks at me, then Raynes. "No more donairs today, please."

The latte is foamy and hot, and the cinnamon bun is sweet without an ounce of a vegan substitute anywhere. I could spend eternity like this.

Raynes gets right down to business. His business, naturally. "Do you agree with Faye?" He senses my confusion. "Her suspect list."

Ahh, the four women in the running for Bedwell's love interest. And murderer, most likely. Three women, actually. Everyone seems to agree Charlene Smith is not in contention for wearing prison orange. I think about the question. It's an important one. "I'd probably reach the same conclusions as Faye. She knows the women better than I do from Norm's perspective."

Raynes wants to run through the pros and cons of each woman from our perspective, and we start with Neela, young(ish), about 32, attractive, and potentially alluring because she is Muslim. She also worked closely with Norm to set up CCC's new online accounting system. I'm also not so sure how religious Norm was. Did he go to church because it was expected of him or because he wanted to?

"So, she's a possible?" I ask for confirmation.

"We may discover they're all possible."

Sure enough. Susan Warrington, at 45, is at least a generation older than Neela, but she is Norm's age, and they share a passion for pastry.

"That was me being petty," I confess to Raynes. HR plays a key role in every department in a company our size, so Susan and Norm would find themselves working together closely and often.

"Did you ever see a spark between him and Susan? Or him and anyone?"

Good grief, a spark. "The only time I ever saw Norm 'sparked' was when there was a danish in the room. And I don't mean a woman from Denmark."

"Still being petty, I see." Raynes takes a jab, but my lack of an answer to his question is apparent.

At 38, Lucy falls between Neela and Susan in age. In terms of attractiveness, she comes in second. Lucy is a small woman with dark black hair that shines no matter the amount of light in a room. She's also diminutive, even dainty. And she's fierce. Lucy's role is to take no crap and to keep CCC from getting into regulatory trouble. That means she is a pain in everyone's side, including mine.

"Some men like that."

I would not have thought Norm was one of them, but apparently, all I know about Norm is his penchant for pastry. Raynes can sense the brick wall before us. "Let's do something else. When was the last time you remember everyone together?"

"The day before Norm died we had a staff meeting."

"Tell me about it."

I think back. "Norm was early. We had danishes."

"You have to let that go." I think Raynes is smiling.

"He was in the room when I arrived and wanted to talk. Then Susan came in."

"Do you think that was planned, like a meet-up?"

I take a few seconds to replay the scene. "I don't think so. I know you're not going to like this, but Norm was focused primarily on pastry."

"What happened when the meeting started?"

"We have an agenda template. Each department provides updates on issues, particularly those that could affect other departments." Something's nagging me though. "I don't recall any important issues. In fact, we got out on time, which is unusual."

"Take a minute." Raynes senses I'm working through something.

"When we were leaving, Neela asked Norm if he had a few minutes to go over the

IT update, and he agreed. I remember he smiled. But mostly, I think it was because there were some danishes left."

Without tangible progress, we continue tossing around probabilities, personalities, and potential passions. At around 6 o'clock, Tiffany sticks her head in the door to say goodbye. Raynes and I decide it's time to order dinner and think of something else.

"I have a suggestion I think you're going to like. More precisely, I think I have a meal you'll like. But let me surprise you."

I'm intrigued. While Raynes orders dinner, I get wine for me and beer for the Nova Scotian. I'm told the only other thing we'll need is napkins. Finger food it is. Dinner arrives about 40 minutes later in a pizza box. Raynes is careful to hide it from me until we dish it up. It resembles slices of beef on a pizza crust with a pepper cream sauce. Real beef. I could live with this man.

But this man has fooled me. One bite lets me know this is not beef and not pepper sauce. It's better. "Oh, my god. I'm in heaven. What in the hell am I eating?"

"Donair pizza." Raynes laughs.

"Take me now." I tilt my head skyward.

There's very little conversation for the next 20 minutes. We stop eating long enough to agree we must eat the entire extra-large pizza before Tiffany gets home, or I will be single before midnight. Somehow coffee following donair pizza doesn't seem right, so I get out the brandy. Raynes raises his left eyebrow. I took that to mean "thank you."

As the brandy swirls in our snifters, I start to rise. "I have something to show you." I say this more to my amazement than his.

We head for the garage. We're not fully through the door when I hear Raynes say, "Holy shit."

I want to think he walks with reverence to my almost-restored (fine, somewhat-restored) 1968 Chevy Camaro. Seeing this car up close and personal is much more impressive than hearing about it from a woman who calls it "the car thing."

"Matador Red. I'm impressed."

"As am I. I figured you were a car guy 'cause of your dad, but if you know the exterior colors, you're a fan."

"My dad dreamed of owning this car, this make and model. Where did you get it?"

"I'm almost embarrassed to say, but I brought it with me when we moved from California."

"Nothing to be embarrassed about. I would sleep with this car."

"Tiffany won't let me," I say, and we both laugh.

For the next hour, we talk cars and examine my '68 Chevy in detail. I appreciate Raynes's appreciation. It's a pleasant evening. I begin to understand why men like to have male friends. We both hear the door open around 9 p.m. Tiffany is back.

As we head back to the house, Raynes puts his hand on my arm. "I'd like to do an exercise with you, but I don't want you to think about your response."

I nod my agreement. Raynes says he will ask me a question, and I have to say the first thing that comes to mind. Easy enough. The first question is, "What's your favorite animal?"

"Dog," I say this quickly and easily.

"Who's the best cook in your house?"

"Me." I smile.

"Who's the best U.S. president?"

"Franklin D. Roosevelt." I'm enjoying this game.

Raynes smiles. Last one. I'm ready. "Who killed Norm Bedwell?"

I don't hesitate. "Lucy Chen." Well, fuck me. Who knew finding a murderer was so simple?

In the end, of course, it's not.

* * *

I'm usually a sound sleeper. Not having to worry about whose feelings I'd hurt, whose caress I was aching for, or whose life was in distress, usually meant I got a solid seven or eight hours. Tonight is not usual.

Perhaps it was the double donair dishes, the car talk, or the Lucy Chen revelation as

Raynes was leaving, but I did not drift off to sleep quickly or easily. I tossed, literally and figuratively, for an hour before my eyes finally closed and stayed closed. Even then my mind was not at ease. I had a dream, something I rarely do or at least something I rarely remember, about eating donairs in my '68 Camaro. I spilled sauce on my pristine cream leather interior and Raynes laughed.

In the dream, I rush to clean up the mess, not angry at the implied ridicule or the potential stain but frustrated. Frustrated at my inability to clean the car. I can't find the disinfecting wipes; the cleaning rags are all dirty; the bucket is just out of reach. I strain to get it off the shelf. It remains firmly beyond my grasp. I yell for Raynes to help. He doesn't respond. I turn toward him, angry, but Raynes is gone.

I'm standing in the middle of the garage surrounded by familiar objects: my car, my tools, and my supplies. But something is wrong. Of course, the stain. I go to find the disinfecting wipes. I fail. I decide to use a rag. All the rags are grimy. I can clean them in the bucket. I see the bucket, and I reach for it. The bucket eludes my grasp. I run around searching for a pole or stick of some kind and spy a broom. I grab it and use the handle to hook the bucket, but the bucket remains firmly entrenched on the shelf.

I can feel myself getting anxious, perhaps even starting to panic. I repeat the sequence to no avail. I shout again for Raynes. He magically appears. "Help me." I sound like I'm pleading.

"I already helped you. I warned you to watch the donair sauce carefully."

I drop my head, and my eyes fix on a spot on the floor. Perhaps this is shame. Raynes is right. He did warn me. He specifically told me what to watch for, and yet I failed to keep my car clean. I realize I'm staring at a piece of paper with something written on it. Without any conscious intent, my left foot slides out to align the piece of paper with the workbench.

I bend down and pick up the piece of paper. It has one word written on it: murderer.

Suddenly, I'm awake. My heart is racing, my pores are sweating, my legs are shaky. I reach for my cell phone to text Raynes. I simply say two words: I know.

The digital clock on my nightstand flashes to a new minute: 5:43. I reach for my phone once more. "Bring Timmies."

* * *

I don't know how the man does it. Within 40 minutes, Raynes is walking through my front door. Every hair is exactly where God ordained; his shirt appears pressed, and he is as relaxed as if going to a weekly brunch date. I'm wearing the same pants I wore yesterday and a sweatshirt from the top of the laundry basket. I'm sure it's clean(ish).

However, I do have a pot of Tiny Footprint's Cold Press Elixir in the French press, ready to drink. Raynes has four different Tim Horton's breakfast sandwiches in a bag. I start with egg, cheese, and sausage in a biscuit. I'm barely through my fist bite when I realize we haven't said a word to each other.

I swallow. "It's the chair, isn't it?"

Raynes smiles, and nods. "It is indeed the chair." He takes a bite of his bagel with bacon and egg. "How did you figure it out?"

"I had a dream I spilled donair sauce on my Camaro and couldn't clean it up. You laughed." Raynes laughs in real life. "You do that a lot."

"Connect the dots for me."

"Something about Norm's office has always bothered me, and you made it clear I should be bothered with your comments about the crime scene. Last night, I realized it's the lone black chair in the center of the room. If you hanged yourself, you would kick over the chair."

"I've thought that from the beginning, but we've known for some time Bedwell was murdered. How does knowing about the chair help identify the murderer?"

"Someone took the time to straighten that chair. It was either important to them because they're anal or they didn't even realize they were doing it."

"Or both." Raynes nods encouragement and leans in. He can sense the climax.

"At CCC, there is only one person I know who would do that." I pause.

"Son of a bitch." A smile hovers. Raynes knows I'm dragging this out just a bit.

"The person who killed Norm Bedwell is … Susan Warrington."

"Son of a bitch."

* * *

Tiffany is up and strolls into the kitchen unaware I'm not at work or that we have company. She takes in my presence first: tousled black hair, sweatshirt, and coffee cup. Then Tiffany sees I'm not alone and nods at Raynes as if it's every day there is a police detective in our kitchen at 7 a.m. I see the smile at the corner of her mouth, but it doesn't have an opportunity to reach its full potential.

The Tim Horton's bags are in plain sight. There are four empty wrappers. "Really. Is this what you do now? Eat bad food and drink good coffee?"

Raynes laughs a hearty baritone sound that fills the kitchen. And as usual, all is forgiven. I'm unsure how to explain the detective's presence, but Raynes handles this. "We think we've had a bit of a breakthrough." He hesitates.

She reads between the lines. "A confidential breakthrough."

"Yes and no. We could be wrong, and there may not be anything to share. If we're right, the question becomes, what to do next? That's what we're going to talk about now."

"Ahh, that's the cue for me to exit." Tiffany reaches inside the fridge and takes out two yogurt parfaits, complete with granola and flax, and places one in front of me and the other in front of Raynes. She takes my coffee cup from me and leaves.

Message received.

While Raynes dutifully eats his blueberry yogurt, I put more coffee in the press and boil the water. I text Marcia, letting her know I'll be late. "The issue," says Raynes as he swallows a last mouthful of yogurt, "is how to prove Warrington killed Bedwell. Neatness is not a crime, nor is it evidence of one."

"What if you brought her in for questioning?"

"That is always an option. I don't know Warrington well enough to know if we're likely to trip her up. I do know if we don't, we've just tipped our hand. Advantage Warrington."

"What would constitute evidence? Aside from the obvious."

"Well, assuming you're right, and I believe you are, we know Warrington didn't physically force Bedwell to put a noose around his neck and climb onto a chair. There were no defensive or other wounds on Bedwell's body."

"She had a gun."

"Or a knife, but likely a gun."

"Where in the hell does a middle-aged HR director get a gun in a country where handguns are illegal?"

"Most likely, it was a shotgun. I'm guessing someone in Susan's family hunts."

"That means she had to bring the shotgun to work, which means she intended to kill Bedwell." I am thinking out loud to myself.

"It's starting to sound premeditated," Raynes agrees, "but it could be that the shotgun was in her car, she and Bedwell get into an argument, and in the heat of the fight, Warrington gets the gun."

"We're assuming she's the love affair." I answer my unasked question. "That makes sense. They're the same age, have work in common, see each other a lot, and obviously confide in one another. As far as I can tell, Warrington was the only one in the office who knew about Bran's bullying, aside from Charlene."

"Now we have a theory and a little circumstantial evidence. We need more."

"How come Warrington's car wasn't in the lot?" I wonder. "We've accounted for all the vehicles that morning."

"I'm guessing Bedwell picked her up somewhere along the way, but there is unlikely to be any camera footage, certainly not that far back."

"To sum up. We have a motive, probably. Ability to commit the crime, yes. Evidence, no. What we need is a confession."

"Any idea how to get one?"

"I just might."

* * *

Something is seriously wrong with me. I've helped the police identify a murderer. Now I'm suggesting I attempt to get that murderer to confess. I recommend having a late talk with Warrington, alone, just the two of us in the office, on some pretense. There is no doubt I am out of my mind.

Raynes does not like my idea, but I notice he doesn't dismiss it outright. His summation, "It's too dangerous. It's too iffy."

I push forward. I can deal effectively with Raynes's second concern. "I know Warrington. I know her well as someone who reports directly to me. I know what buttons to push. She's more likely to slip up or open up with me."

That argument, of course, leads directly to Raynes's top concern. I could get hurt or worse.

I'd wear a wire, and Raynes and his team would be nearby. What could go wrong?

Plenty according to the detective sipping coffee across from me in my breakfast nook. Warrington could have a gun; she could be unhinged. And no matter how fast Raynes et al could get to me, they couldn't outrun a firearm.

I point out Warrington is not unhinged. Indeed, the calculated nature of her crime has made catching her most difficult. Also, I point out that I can wear a vest. I have seen this on *Blue Bloods*.

Raynes is relenting. Then he throws his most deadly volley. "What do we tell Tiffany?"

* * *

It's decided I wear a wire. Raynes and his crew will wait down the hall in what appears to be an empty office. I'll push to get Susan to open up initially by appealing to her heartbroken side. She has, after all, witnessed the death of her lover. Admittedly, she caused that death.

If empathy doesn't work, and undeniably this will be a stretch for me, I might be able to frighten her into tripping up by perhaps hinting the cops are close to making an arrest. Raynes and I will develop a loose script. He seems to understand where I'll need nudging.

We also agree on the question of Tiffany. My wife is not to know anything about this.

That, as it turns out, was a very, very bad decision.

Chapter 13

The date is set for next Tuesday evening when Michael Graves has his weekly hockey game and, therefore, can't be invited to join us for a last-minute meeting. That gives us five days to prep me and set up logistics.

I'll ask Susan if she can stay to discuss a few issues, including the ongoing audit. That may raise an eyebrow, but only slightly. It's not unusual for some or all of us to stay after hours, depending on the critical matters we're discussing. And with everything going on at CCC now, HR plays a key role. That said, it's unlikely anyone else will be around later on a Tuesday night. Even if they are, it won't be a problem. Susan and I will meet in my office, which is set off from the other offices on the executive floor.

Getting Raynes and his team inside the building unseen may be slightly more challenging. It's decided I'll order something for dinner, make this a working meeting over the supper hour. I'll ask Susan if she minds picking up the order. In fact, I may even get Tiffany to drive me to work in the morning using some excuse. Then I can honestly tell Susan that I don't have my car with me.

To account for the pre-meeting prep-time absences from home, Raynes will "invite" me to a local soccer tournament over the weekend. Tiffany will be thrilled I have bro time, and since the "tournament" involves more than one game, several absences will not seem unusual.

Raynes and I are having coffee at Timmy's and eating something called Timbiebs. What happens when Justin Bieber goes corporate sponsorship. The bite-sized doughnuts come in weird flavors, including sour cream chocolate chip and birthday cake waffle. I'm on my fourth one.

"How are you dealing with all this?"

"To be honest," I say between bieb bites, "I'm thinking about a donair." That gets me the laugh I expected. "I'm fine." I'm being honest and don't think anything will go wrong. I know Susan Warrington, I know myself, and Raynes. We have this aced.

I couldn't have been more wrong.

* * *

It's 11 a.m. by the time I get to the office. Marcia doesn't blink at the hiccup in our routine. I get a quick update on what's happened in my absence and prepare to do some real work. I'm sure the senator would be proud.

I'm midway through the first stack of papers on my desk when Marcia lets me know Zahra Bashir has called. Marcia told her I was in meetings most of the day, but she would pass the message along. I wonder why Bashir hadn't contacted me directly. When I check my cell phone, I discover she had three times. I forgot I'd put the phone on silent when meeting with Raynes.

Marcia remains standing in the doorway, waiting for any instructions. "I'll call her directly." Normally, I would ignore this message and reach out to Thorne for a strategy briefing, but the timing has me a little unnerved. We're on the cusp of catching a killer and CCN calls.

As usual, Bashir is breezy and pleasant when she answers. "Thank you so much for getting back to me. I was hoping you might be available for an interview on Monday. We're doing a piece on the Halifax economy and wanted to speak with someone in the cannabis sector."

"That's a great topic." I hope I sound more believable than she does. "I'm between meetings at the moment. Can I call you later when I have a better sense of what Monday looks like?"

"I'd appreciate it. I'll need to finalize the line-up by 3 p.m."

I promise her I'll let her know before then. My next two calls are to Raynes and

Thorne, in that order. Raynes doesn't see a conflict, and if questions are posed about the murder, I can say I can't comment while the police are investigating the matter. Thorne agrees but thinks the interview opportunity is good because it positions the cannabis sector as a mainstream business.

Great, that means I have to call the senator.

For some reason I've never fathomed, Senator John Williams is always available to take my calls. Does the man not have to attend senate sessions? Or run committee meetings? Make illicit deals? Apparently, not.

"Now, what's gone wrong?" he snaps before I can say, "Hello."

I'm tempted to respond by saying, "Tiffany and I are fine. Thanks for asking." I resist the temptation. "I wanted to let you know CCN has called asking for an interview on Monday. They're doing a piece on the healthy Halifax economy and wanted to speak with someone in the cannabis sector."

"Well, that's a chunderfuck." Obviously, the word has caught on. I must find out what it means and thank David Clements for gifting the American language with a new curse word. I guess I'll hear a lot of this in my future.

"What did you tell them?" It sounds like a question, but it's more of a bark, bringing me back to the present.

I'm not falling for this. It's a trap. Say "yes," and you're opening the company up to embarrassment. Say "no," and you're missing out on a significant opportunity. "Thorne and I both feel this could be good for our reputation and that of the industry."

There's a slight pause. "I agree."

I check my pulse to make sure I'm alive. "I'll set a time and keep you posted."

"You're doing a good job, Riel." Okay, something is seriously wrong. Maybe my father-in-law has a terminal illness. Or, and it takes me a second or two, he's spoken with Tiffany who has told him to be nice to me. Still, the man is trying.

I have no idea where the next words out of my mouth come from. Perhaps it's the unusual context I'm finding myself in or the need to get the senator firmly on my side for my presidential ambitions. Either way, my lips parted, and these words tumbled out, "John, everything is good here. Tiffany and I are fine. But in case anything should go off the rails, I might text you a word. If you get that word, please call Tiffany right away and tell her to call Detective Raynes."

I know the senator has a thousand questions, the first of which must be, "Are you nuts?" To his credit, he pushes those questions into some recess of his mind. "What's the word?"

It takes me only a second. "Chunderfuck."

* * *

Surprisingly, I get some CCC work done. I spent most of the afternoon with Delroy Brown, operations director, reviewing options for new strains and increased production.

It's decided we'll run with a Nova Scotia theme. It's a little brazen of us; we'll have to stay firmly within the Health Canada regulations for the promotion of weed. Anything that appeals to young people is verboten. But something like "Bluenose Breeze" should be allowable. Of course, then we need permission to use "Bluenose," the name of Nova Scotia's revered schooner.

Delroy and I agree we need to bring in marketing at this point. He'll call our agency, Quantum Communications, and set an appointment for next week. And that's a wrap.

It's almost 6 p.m. I gather up some work to take home and file a few documents lying on my desk. I'm somewhat looking forward to meeting with Raynes tomorrow, and I'm somewhat dreading it.

I feel her presence before I see her; I take my eyes off my screen. Susan Warrington is standing in the doorway. "Do you need something?" I know I sound natural. I'm good at this. Pretending I care, pretending I'm just like everyone else.

"Do you have a few minutes? There are a few issues I'd like to wrap up before next week."

So, it's Friday night and Susan wants to chat. I'm determining if this is normal or if something is up, and I need to do that in the few split seconds before I have to answer. "I was just packing up for the week."

"This won't take long." Warrington: 1.

"Come on in."

The admin building has been emptied by now. It's dark outside. I'm reminded of trailers for horror movies I never watched. Susan seems on edge, but I tell myself it's not unusual in the presence of one's CEO or when broaching a difficult topic.

"I think it's time to open up Norm's office," Susan says in a rush of breath. "We need to get back to normal. As much as we can."

I'm somewhat stunned. "You mean Norm's office is sealed?"

Susan takes it as a rebuke.

Not intended that way, so I apologize for my tone. "I assumed we had cleared out Norm's office for the auditor."

"She's been working in one of the meeting rooms or at her office offsite. I haven't had the heart to dismantle Norm's office, but the longer we wait, the more attention we draw to the fact that we haven't touched anything since his death." Her last few words are hastily said as if they have left an unpleasant aftertaste in her mouth.

"Would it take much to dismantle?"

"Yes and no." Susan suggests we start with a clean slate. Remove all of Norm's furniture and belongings. Anything the family might want, they can have. Anything else can go to goodwill.

"Goodbye, Norm," I say, almost to myself.

Again, Susan takes this as a rebuke.

I reassure her it isn't intended that way. I agree with her plan. "How do we do this?"

"I don't mind doing it. It should be someone who knew Norm, out of respect. I could come in this weekend, and everything would be gone by Monday."

There it is, the reason for this little tête à tête. "I should probably check with Detective Raynes."

Susan looks up quickly. "Why? The police have cleared the scene." She catches my wry grin. "Their language, not mine."

"I thought it might show we are being considerate, ensuring nothing can compromise the investigation." And now we are in it. The opportunity has knocked.

I open the door. "I feel the police are close to an arrest."

"What do you mean?" Susan is taken aback. I remind myself this pronouncement would have a similar effect on most people, me included.

"Detective Raynes has been in touch several times, asking pointed questions." We're in it now; there's nothing to do but continue.

"What kinds of questions?"

I evade the issue, at least for now. "You know, now that I think of it, Detective Raynes would have been better off asking you some of those questions than me." I see the scowl and what I believe is a hint of suspicion. Perhaps I've gone too far too quickly. "I mean, after all, you knew about Bran's bullying. Norm obviously trusted your judgment."

"What kind of questions?" Susan persists.

"There was a strange one about bowling." I'm stalling. "I get the feeling that did not lead the police in the direction they wanted."

"Norm didn't bowl," Susan says matter-of-factly.

"I told them I didn't think he did."

I can't tell if Susan heard me. It's almost like I can see the wheels spinning in her mind. "Why didn't they just ask Faye?"

So, my HR director is intelligent and fast. "They might have. Perhaps they were confirming the information or …"

"Or what?" Susan presses.

If I go here, there is no turning back. I plunge. "Or they think there were things Norm was keeping from Faye."

"What would Norm keep from Faye?"

She knows playing clueless isn't working.

"The obvious," I say. There is a hint of a sneer. I do not like being treated like a fool.

"They think there is another woman?" It's more of a statement but nothing close to an admission.

"They do indeed." I wonder how far I should go with this. I push. "I get the distinct feeling they think it's someone who works here."

Now I see her shock tinged with something else: fear. "Did they say whom?" She can't hide the tremor in her voice.

"They didn't, but Detective Raynes asked me several questions about Lucy Chen." I am also playing clueless. "I'm telling you this in confidence."

"Of course." Susan's hand absently reaches to straighten the files on my desk. "Do you think Lucy and Norm were having an affair?"

Not the question I was expecting, but it lets me know what is important to Susan. I can use that. "To be honest, I couldn't see Norm having an affair with anyone and certainly not anyone in this office."

"Is that what you told Detective Raynes?"

"In a round-about way." I am making shit up as the conversation moves forward. "He didn't ask me outright. I'm reading between the lines." I hope this will give me some leeway if this discussion doesn't go as planned.

It doesn't. "If Norm were having an affair, who do you think he'd fall for?" Again, not the question I was expecting. I'm feeling less confident I'm in control of this conversation.

"Charlene Smith," I say with what I believe is no hesitation.

"She's gay," Susan fires back. Her tone is neutral; nothing else about her body language is.

"I know that now. I didn't know it when Norm was killed."

"Let's play 'pick a murderer.'" Susan is making light of this. She's failing. I don't think I'm going to like this game.

I attempt to turn the tables. "You knew Norm better than me. Who would you pick?"

Susan isn't falling for my deflection. "Think about when you saw Norm happiest."

"When he had a danish," I answer without thinking. Susan stands up. Now I've pissed her off. I'm assuming our conversation is over. I'm wrong.

"This focus on Norm has gone on far too long. I think we can resolve this tonight. Wait here. I'll be right back."

She's gone before I can lift my gaping jaw back into place. I'm not sure what Susan has in mind, but I'm sure I will not like it. I'm wondering if I have time to text Raynes. I don't.

My HR director is back within what seems like mere seconds, and she is not alone. She's brought along a buddy. "Let me introduce you to my dear friend, Beanie." Susan is pointing a rifle at my chest. I attempt to interject. Now I fail. "Her full name is Beanfield Sniper Remington Sendero SF II. But no matter what you call her, she's deadly. Just ask Norm."

I'm trying to figure out my exit strategy, at least one that keeps me alive. I opt, badly, for de-escalation. "Susan, what the fuck are you doing? What the fuck are you talking about? Norm wasn't shot."

"No. He wasn't shot." I swear the woman is enjoying herself.

I don't know where to go from here. Susan picks up the thread for me. She's not into de-escalation apparently. "Do you think I'm fucking stupid?"

The question takes me back. I hope Susan will interpret this as meaning, "How could anyone think you're stupid." It seems she doesn't.

"You sit here, you smug little bastard, playing some stupid game of 'I know what you did.' Do you think I can't see right through that little ploy?"

Smug? I'm offended. I work very hard to appear approachable and sincere. I must chat with Tiffany about these attributes. First, I'll need to get past the loon and her steely girlfriend. "Susan, there is no ploy," I assure her.

"You're a terrible liar."

Now I'm pissed. I'm a great liar. It's a skill I practice. She's just shooting blanks. Metaphorically, of course. "I don't understand what you are so upset about."

"Truly terrible."

Okay, fuck it. "So why did you kill Norm?"

Susan can sense my anger. "Ahh, there he is. Honest Abe. Let's get down to it. We'll play 20 questions. You first."

And I'm the psychopath. "Fine. Why did you kill Norm?"

"He wanted to go back to Faye, snivelling little Faye. He wanted to unite his family and spend time with his son, with the woman who gave birth to his son. His words. Although, those may have been his last words." Susan answers calmly. I swear she is grinning.

"But why kill him?" It's a stupid question. Sitting here with this woman and her gun, I understand the urge. I want to take Susan Warrington's skull and smash it repeatedly against any hard surface, again and again. But then there is Beanie.

"That's two questions." You have to give Susan points for accuracy. "My turn. How did the cops figure out it was me?"

"The chair."

"What fucking chair?" Susan does not ask politely. Beanie bobs in the air.

"In the middle of the room. It was upright."

"Who doesn't pick up a chair from the floor?"

"A dead man," I reply as cool as a cuke. "And that's two questions. My turn."

"You're out of questions," Susan snaps. "Now you're going to meet the same fate as my dear departed Norman." She grabs a chair from across the room and tosses it toward the center of my office. "Get up." She waves Beanie in the direction of the newly positioned chair.

Now I see why Norm would hang himself. Beanie is a powerful persuader. I move slowly, thinking of a way out of this. I opt for the obvious. "The cops aren't going to buy this, especially detective Raynes. It will look like what it is, two staged suicides."

"This one will be different because you're going to write a suicide note. You're going to confess to killing Norm Bedwell."

Not bad at all. The woman is fast on her feet, or maybe she has been coming up with a Plan B all along. "And why would I kill Norm?"

"Financial irregularities. You've been dipping your fingers where they don't belong."

That could work if Susan had picked anyone but me to play confessor. Raynes will never buy my guilt, and the cops have audited our financials, but Susan doesn't know that. Now I need a Plan B. "You kill me here, and it's the end of CCC."

"Who gives a shit?" Susan snarls. "This place is a drug-infested mess."

I resent that on both counts. This is a well-run company, the largest cannabis producer in Atlantic Canada and the third largest in the country. Our profits grow double digits yearly and some little HR turd thinks she can malign what I've built. Now I want to snarl. I resist the urge. "If I die somewhere else, CCC survives, and we'll need a new CEO."

"Yippie." Beanie is in full motion as I move toward the chair, slowly, very slowly.

"Who do you think they'll appoint?" Now I have her attention. "You're the logical choice. Michael's too young; Neela's too IT-focused. Delroy has no experience outside operations, and Lucy has had to remain at arm's length from the company to maintain objectivity. You're CCC's new CEO."

I can see Susan likes the idea. "So, you need to die somewhere else."

I've bought some time. I'm rapidly going through death scenes. Got it. "There's a cabin Tiffany and I went to last year. Remote. It will be closed this time of year. We can easily break in."

"Good place for a man to kill himself," says Susan, mostly to herself. "Where is it?"

"It's along the Northumberland shore, about 90 minutes from here. Fàilte Cottages." Tiffany and I have been there. Fàilte means "welcome" in Scot Gaelic, so we called the spot our *welcome home*. It was a private joke. My first name is French, my last name Spanish, and Tiffany is 100% WASP American. We thought it ironic that the cottage was rooted in Gaelic.

Like it matters now. Susan and Beanie are at the helm, and no one knows where the hell we'll end up. I'm only hoping I'm breathing.

"We'll take my car," Susan says. "I've had the GPS disabled."

I'm thinking madly. I've talked myself into an additional hour and a half of breathing time, a little more if I stall, but I'd prefer a lifetime. I need to alert Raynes. "I'd better use the washroom first."

Susan isn't stupid. She comes to the washroom with me and takes my phone before I enter. So that plan won't work. We're back in my office. I have my coat and gloves, and Susan and Beanie are good to go.

"I have to tell Tiffany something." I can hear the pleading in my voice.

"No, you don't." Beanie nudges me forward.

"If I don't show up for supper or answer the phone, Tiffany will have cops crawling all over this place and this province."

"No, she won't. Nice try."

"Have you met my wife?"

That stops the dynamic duo in their tracks. "You can text her, and I want to read the message before you send it."

I'm thinking of what I can say to Tiffany to give her a head's up that I need help without giving Batshit Crazy a head's up at the same time. I hope this works: *Tiff, I have to leave you. Please dont come looking for me. I'm the one who killed Norm Bedwell and I need to get away before the police catch me. Please dont contact Franklin Raynes. There is nothing I wish more than to here you say, "Welcome home." I love you. Tell your father Chunderfuck for me.*

Batshit grabs the phone from my hands. She doesn't pick up on my use of "Tiff," or "Franklin," names I never use. She also misses "dont," a grammatical mistake I would never make. She does catch "here," but doesn't seem to care. It only seems to reinforce my uselessness in her eyes.

What the well-armed HR director does catch is "Chunderfuck." "What's this?"

"I don't know," I say honestly. "It's a word my father-in-law uses. He'll see it as a term of affection, our final goodbye."

Batshit doesn't appear to buy this, but she shrugs. "This will be all over soon. If it's code, it'll be too late for the big U.S. senator to save you."

I'm hoping she's wrong and as soon as Tiffany gets the text, she'll call Raynes and her father. I'm hoping the cops will be on the road within several minutes of us. I'm hoping Tiffany will check her texts. I'm hoping Tiffany isn't in the middle of a yoga practice. "Dear God, read your messages, Tiffany."

We're on the Trans Canada heading north toward Pictou on the 102. There is no stalling on the main highway, with four lanes and fewer vehicles. I dragged out getting gas as long as I reasonably could, but I am now doing a steady 100 km an hour. We'll turn off onto one of the trunk roads in about an hour. It will be darker, windier, and bumpier. I may add time to our travels then.

Batshit wants to talk. More precisely, she wants to gloat. "You thought you were going to take me down, you pissant you."

I do want to kill this woman. I want to push the gas pedal to the floor, swerve the car into the woods that border the 102, and watch this woman die a painfully slow death. Unfortunately, I'd likely die as well. Not a great plan.

I grit every tooth I have. "Why kill Norm?" If I keep her talking, she may not notice my attempts to delay our arrival. And what does she have to lose with Beanie by her side? Apparently, nothing.

"I told you. Norm thought he could go back to his wife and his beloved Bran. I thought otherwise."

"But why kill Norm in the office? Why make a public spectacle out of it?" I'm honestly curious.

"How would you have done it?" It's more of a challenge than a question.

I rise to the challenge. "I'd have invited him for a drink in my office after work. I'd have spiked his drink, waited for him to get wobbly, then walked him to my car. At that point, I have all the time I need to finish him off and hide the body."

"That presumes this was premeditated," Batshit says. The gloating is back, and with good reason.

"Wasn't it?" I counter.

Batshit hesitates. I'm unsure if she's considering what the honest answer is or whether to tell me the truth. The urge to gloat wins out again. "It was."

I turn to her perplexed. "Why?"

"Okay, pretty boy, I'll tell you why. I don't look like you; I'm not charming like you; I don't exude charisma like you. Norm was my last chance at love, and it was wonderful. When he called us off, I refused to go gently into the next chapter of my life."

"What did you do?" I must admit she has me hooked.

"I told Norm in my sweetest HR voice that I understood his decision completely. In fact, I agreed with it. Family is everything. You know, shit like that."

I do, indeed. It is the bread on which politicians spread their butter.

Batshit is on a roll. There is no stopping her now. "I waited a few days, always being cordial and professional. The fool bought it hook, line, and sinker. On Tuesday, I asked Norm, as a friend, of course, if he would pick me up at the garage on his way into work the next day. My car needed maintenance. I apologized profusely for the early hour."

"So, you came to work together. Ergo, your car isn't in the lot." I am thinking out loud.

"Ergo." Batshit laughs.

"And the gun?"

"In my gym bag."

And there it is, Murder 101.

"Where are we?" Batshit peers out the window, hadn't realized we'd left the highway or that I've been heading in the wrong direction toward Amherst and the New Brunswick border. Of course, it won't take her long to figure out we're lost or I'm manipulating her, but every minute counts.

"We're on the 104." I pretend that answers her question.

It doesn't. Batshit sits straight up, peering out at the surroundings. It's pitch black, darker than the highway, with fewer lights. There is only a smattering of people in the houses and cottages on the back road. But there is government signage. As we round a bend in the road, Batshit realizes we are driving south, opposite where we should be headed.

"I will blow your brains out right now." I think she means it. I turn the car around at the first spot to allow a U-turn. I'm done stalling. Batshit is on full alert. I figure I've given Raynes an extra 40 minutes to save my life when all the delays add up.

Please, Tiffany, check your damn phone.

I get a little lost as we approach the road to Fàilte Cottages. It's so dark, like driving through an onyx, and only a simple, unlit sign shows us we have reached our destination. The winding road goes between a grove of pine and spruce trees, adding to the darkness, and the eeriness. I park at the top of the gravel road. The cottages are about 50 feet away.

"Get out." Batshit barks, stating the obvious. "And don't think about making a run for it. I will shoot at anything that moves."

I had contemplated hightailing it. When I open my car door, it will be the only time she doesn't have the damn gun trained directly on me. I can't see a foot in front of my face. Batshit has her phone's flashlight on. Beanie directs me to stand in front of her. I obey.

Images of Susan Warrington badly mutilated and in excruciating pain fill my mind. I see limbs ripped from her body, gaping holes in her torso, and bits of brain beside her dying body. I find myself comforted. It may be better than meditation.

By now, I'm directly in front of Batshit, and we are steps away from the front door of the first cottage. "It has to be the third cottage," I tell her. "That's the one Tiffany and I stayed in."

Well, that bought me another 50 feet. I find myself wondering how many centimetres 50 feet is. Obviously, impending death affects one's sanity. I hear a twig snap, and hope springs eternal.

Batshit hears it, too. She swings around, aiming Beanie somewhere in the starless night. At this point, any NCIS team would tackle the killer to the ground, rendering her immobile. I remain stock-still and understand why I am not in law enforcement.

Batshit is so quiet I think for a second she's not breathing. Wouldn't that be great. But in a few seconds she turns, and Beanie nestles into my lower back again. "Fuckin' nature."

"It was just a raccoon." I say this almost calmly as if I know about raccoons' nocturnal habits.

I'm about to put a foot on the first step to my demise when a voice says in my ear, "Drop the gun, or I will blow your fuckin' brains all over this place. For the racoons."

I know this voice. Something in my chest stops straining to leave my body. I feel my muscles unclench as I turn my body ever so slightly.

Lin Raynes is standing behind Batshit. I later learned he planted the business end of a SIG Sauer P226, standard issue for Halifax police officers, firmly between her T10 and T11 vertebra.

The entire area gets flooded with light from flashlights and headlights, like a disco party on the set of *Footloose*.

"Get on your fuckin' knees," Raynes says. I start to bend and can hear his laugh echo across Fàilte Cottages. I'm so happy I could dance.

One of the six RCMP officers in the detective's entourage removed Beanie. Batshit drops to her knees, none too gently helped by Raynes. As Raynes leans down to cuff Warrington, now seemingly harmless and innocuous, he looks at me. "You okay?"

"Peachy. Nice night for a nature walk."

The laughter is back. "You had better call Tiffany." He tosses me his phone.

Before the first ring fades, Tiffany answers. "I'm okay. I'm fine," I blurt out before she has time to say, "Hello."

I'm expecting tears, wailing, effusive love whispers. My wife simply says, "Come home."

I can't get there fast enough.

Chapter 14

We're pulling out of the cottage roadway heading for home. I want to hear how Raynes got here. I know I'll have to tell my story, likely repeatedly, but first, I'd like to fill in the blanks that saved my life.

"I take it Tiffany decoded my message."

"Took her all of four seconds." Raynes is smiling. "You have one helluva wife. She's on the phone with me, telling me to head to Fàilte Cottages in Pictou. You're in danger. I'm to call the RCMP en route, and she'll call me back once she's talked to her father."

Usually Raynes would need more details, he says, but the urgency in Tiffany's voice got him moving. Ten minutes later, she's back on the phone with him, explaining the text and how it wasn't what appeared on the surface. "I told her about our plan to trap Warrington. Said you must have grabbed an opportunity that presented itself."

Raynes hesitates. "At some point, you will be in big trouble for that. Tonight, you're probably fine." He glances my way. "Nice touch about the senator."

"Don't know why I ever did that. Just immensely glad I did."

I have to relive my evening with Batshit for Raynes. It takes up most of the drive home. The detective doesn't ask many questions. When he does, they're pointed and on point. My powers of observation have been honed over decades of being different and not wanting to be found out, so I'm able to provide a detailed report of what happened and what was said. There's a detached feel to the report as if I'm talking about someone else. It's normal for me.

Raynes shifts in his seat. "You know you'll have to repeat all of this in a formal statement."

I nod. "With pleasure. Anything I can do so that woman never experiences freedom again."

"That's likely, given her age and the fact the crime was premeditated."

Batshit's legal prognosis gives me great comfort. I sense Raynes peering at me and try to wipe the smile from my face.

He grins in response. "I'm going to switch positions."

"You want me to drive?" I ask, a little stunned.

Raynes laughs. It's a loud, deep belly hoot, and I find myself laughing along with him. "What I meant is, I'm going to put my detective shield away and ask you something, not as a cop, but as a friend."

I'm hoping he can't read the shock on my face. It never occurred to me that this man and I were friends. I don't have friends. At least, I don't remember having friends. I must ask Tiffany about this.

"Two questions." Raynes focuses on the road ahead. "Are you really okay?"

I can tell the question is genuine and personal; I give it the consideration it deserves. It's been a harrowing night, but somewhere at the back of my mind, I don't believe I ever thought I'd die or even that Batshit would somehow come out on top. Was I scared? Yep. But I think I was more pissed. It's a different kind of adrenaline.

"You know what, I am fine," I say after a minute or two. "Do I ever want to go through an experience like this again? No. Will it fundamentally change who I am? No. Will it have a pronounced effect on my life? No."

"So, okay."

I grin in response. Question two comes out of nowhere and is about as perfect as possible.

"Do you want a donair?"

Maybe Raynes is right. Maybe this man is my friend.

* * *

Before we get to my house, Raynes tells me Faye Bedwell is there. "I asked her to come over to keep Tiffany company."

I take a meditative breath to absorb this. Why would Tiffany need company? She'd be worried, naturally. But Raynes could call her and let her know how things were going. Unless they weren't going well. So, this is Raynes protecting my wife.

"Thank you. But why Faye Bedwell?"

"I didn't know anyone else. I also thought I could update Mrs. Bedwell if necessary. It will be hard on her and Bran, and it will go public."

Going public means I'll have to call the senator and Clements. Dammit all to hell.

* * *

Weeping and clutching were what I expected from Tiffany when I walked up to our house. Instead, I got a whirlwind of blond hair and blue jeans, hurling herself at me before I was through the door. Tiffany didn't say a word. She simply clung.

While I couldn't connect with the emotions, I can understand fear, especially now, and I understand loss. I realized how hard the last five hours must have been for Tiffany. Her life here is built around me and my work. It's not her country, her profession, or her career path. Her family is not here. It's me. I'm Tiffany's equator, and someone wanted to implode her world.

I realize Tiffany has stopped clinging. She's sniffing. Two piercing blue eyes are staring at me. "You smell funny."

Raynes tries to say something about nature and the natural aroma of Pictou County. Tiffany is having none of this. She turns to me, then Raynes. I believe our heads are hanging.

"Son of a bitch," says my always elegant and refined wife. "You stopped for a donair. You nearly die and leave me quaking with fear, yet you have time to eat a helpless animal?" Tiffany is pissed.

I have nothing for her. "I didn't have supper," I offer up by way of explanation. I should have kept my mouth shut.

I can see the hand as it cuts the air and aims for my upper arm. It's not intended to hurt but to reprimand. And suddenly, there is the weeping and clutching I had expected. "It's all right." I kiss the top of my wife's head and rub her back lightly. "I'm fine. We're fine."

Faye Bedwell moves forward silently, almost invisibly. She expertly extricates my wife from the ninja grip she has on my body. "Why don't we make some of that lovely coffee Riel likes so much?"

I'm impressed and confused. I shoot Raynes a glance as the two women make their way to the kitchen.

"Normal reaction to trauma. I see it all the time."

The coffee is a pleasant treat: Kopi luwak. What many critics crudely refer to as "cat poop coffee" is an Indonesian bean famous for being ingested by the palm civet. The result is an exquisite deep roast with hints of plum and rose. I'm savouring the aroma until I catch Tiffany staring at me. Perhaps now is not a good time to sniff.

Raynes catches the exchange and laughs.

Tiffany silences him with a single look. "Tell me everything," she says.

I don't. I omit the scary bits and downplay Beanie's role.

"So, basically, this was a fun road trip with a colleague," Tiffany says. I am reminded, yet again, that my wife is very bright.

We do the Raynes-laughs-Tiffany-glowers thing again. Using my Thorne media training, I deflect. "Bottom line: everyone is safe, and Susan Warrington is safely in jail. But there are some unpleasant realities ahead."

That seems to do the trick. Raynes looks at Faye Bedwell. "Warrington's arrest will become public. Sooner than later, I imagine."

"I'll prepare Bran," she says. "We'll get through this. And I'm glad the woman is where she belongs."

"I called her 'Batshit' in my mind," I say. I have no idea why, but it appears to be the right thing to have said. Everyone is laughing.

Tiffany reaches into the freezer for a homemade blueberry grunt she purchased at a local craft fair, and second cups of coffee are poured.

There's a warmth in the room. And all it took was me nearly dying.

* * *

I spent most of the next day focused on the fallout from Batshit. If I'm not at the police station giving a statement, signing a statement, or answering questions related to Norm Bedwell's death and Susan Warrington's movements, I'm with Thorne prepping for the media onslaught.

Late on Saturday, Tiffany suggests we drop by the Bedwells. She has an apple pie. I don't know why we would do this, but I trust Tiffany's judgment. Faye sounds pleased that I've called to suggest we interrupt her weekend.

There's a pot of Morses on the stove when we arrive. Bran has a school project for English he wants to show me. It's about zombies. I'm trying to connect literature with a love of the dead. Shit, I guess I just did.

When we return to the living room, even I can sense something is up. Bran looks at his mother as she says, "Honey, there is something I need to tell you. It's good news, but it isn't all good news."

I feel a small hand reach inside mine. "Let's sit down," I say. "We'll have some pie

287

and ice cream, and we'll talk this through. Like adults."

Bran stands taller. Faye and Tiffany give me big smiles. I must ask Tiffany later why they did that. Faye explains that Norm's killer has been caught. She tells him it was someone that Norm worked with and someone that Norm had a relationship with.

"What do you mean 'relationship'?" Bran asks.

Faye fumbles through an explanation with a little help from Tiffany. Bran is not buying this. "Dad didn't love us?"

I can see the concern on Tiffany's face. I assume that must be pain etched on Faye's. "Just the opposite," I say. I must learn to keep my mouth shut.

Bran turns to me. "What do you mean?"

"What your mother and my wife haven't told you is that Susan Warrington pulled a gun on me last night. We drove to Pictou. She was running away from what she'd done."

"Are you all right?" Bran asks, and I am confronted with the reality that this little boy cares about me. Goddammit.

I reach for his shoulder. "I'm fine. I'm really fine. But when you spend two hours in a car with someone like this woman, you find out stuff. Want to know what I found out?"

"Yes." Bran is leaning forward, hanging on to me and what I have to say. So are Tiffany and Faye.

"Your dad was killed because he told this woman he loved you and your mom too much to ever do anything to hurt you. He wanted nothing more to do with her and everything to do with his family."

"Motherfucker!" That was from the 11-year-old in the room. I can see the shock on Faye's and Tiffany's faces. I'm impressed. Apparently, I shouldn't be.

"Bran Bedwell, language!" his mother says. There is a hint of pride.

It doesn't seem to matter now. Bran has wormed his way under my arms, shoulders, and other body parts until we are wedged tightly together. I realize he's crying.

"Thank you," he mumbles.

* * *

I sleep like a very happy baby. Once under the covers, it takes several minutes to extricate myself from Tiffany's grip, but as soon as she snores softly on her side of the bed, I'm dead to the world. At 6 a.m., I'm wide awake. I know my body well enough to know when it's ready to move. I get up and head for the kitchen. The aroma of my Nicaraguan medium roast is filling up the kitchen, and I'm savouring the scent when I receive a text message from Raynes.

On my way. I have breakfast. For Tiffany too.

I'm too content to object. Too relaxed to be curious. It's nice to be alive.

About 20 minutes later, the 6'4" detective saunters into my kitchen like it's his second home. He's got four breakfast sandwiches from Timmys. He's also got breakfast for Tiffany. Some vegan/vegetarian thing with potatoes and kale and a sauce that is supposed to resemble gravy. I think I love this man.

I'm midway through my second sandwich, sausage, egg, and cheese on a biscuit when Tiffany walks into the kitchen. She's automatically reaching for the French press before it registers that Raynes has joined us. She smiles, but it's short-lived.

She spies the crumpled wrapping paper, and dammit if she doesn't arch her left eyebrow. "Anything you'd like to share?"

I feel the temperature in the room drop.

"I have breakfast for you," says Raynes, reaching for the green and white blob. "Got it from Heartwood." Heartwood is a popular vegetarian restaurant in Halifax.

The smile is back. "How sweet."

"It's a blob," I point out.

"It's my blob," she says, "and it's very sweet."

Now Raynes is smiling. Good grief.

Tiffany joins us for breakfast. She slides into the chair next to me and starts chatting with Raynes. It's a natural movement, and it implies this is all routine. Then again, perhaps it is.

Once the blob is gone, devoured, truth be told, Tiffany pours a second cup of the Nicaraguan brew and starts to rise.

"Don't go on my account," says Raynes.

Tiffany and I are surprised. We'd both assumed he was here on business.

"I do have to discuss a few things with Riel," says Raynes reading our minds and faces, "but nothing confidential or potentially lethal."

Tiffany shoots Raynes a look. It's not warm. Maybe it's too soon?

We're all settled, well-fed, and caffeinated. Raynes changes tone. "Warrington has confessed. Truth is, she's bragged about how clever she is, about how she committed the perfect murder, about how no man will ever toss her aside. It's enough to put her away for first-degree murder."

I learned in the last day that first-degree murder in Canada is a premeditated act and carries a minimum 25-year sentence. There is no death penalty in this country.

"That means there won't be a trial?" Tiffany asks.

"Warrington has signed a statement and agreed to a life sentence. It's over," says Raynes.

Both Tiffany and I grin. It's good news, but I should have known not to get ahead of myself.

"I wanted to give you a head's up," Raynes continues. "We're going to hold a press conference tomorrow morning to announce Norm Bedwell's killer has been caught."

So, I'll be on the phone for part of today with my regulator and my father-in-law.

"It's a way to deal with all the media interest at one time, and it lets us toot our horn," says Raynes.

I have questions for myself and Raynes when my cell phone rings. It's Marcia. Marcia never calls me at home. And I was so close to a zen-like state at 6 a.m.

"I'm sorry to interrupt your Sunday morning. I wanted to remind you about your interview with Zahra Bashir tomorrow."

Crap. I had forgotten all about the interview. "I'll have to cancel, but I should do that myself. Thank you for the reminder."

"Glad to help," says Marcia, but she doesn't hang up.

That's my cue. "There is something I should tell you. They have arrested Norm Bedwell's murderer. It's Susan Warrington."

Silence. I'm uncertain if Marcia is shocked or reassured. Her sixth sense is as sharp as ever. "Are you all right?"

"I am." Tiffany catches my eye and gives me the head tilt. "Thank you for asking," I say. "There is something you can do." I put the call on speaker.

I tell her about the news conference and the need to meet with the executive team before that. We'll watch the conference together in the boardroom. Marcia will send an email first thing in the morning and make it as neutral as a mandatory meeting can be.

"What would you like me to do with Warrington's office?"

Raynes tells me they would like to go through the office for corroborating evidence, but there is no rush. The police secured the office on the weekend. He agrees there is no need for crime scene tape, but the door needs to remain firmly locked.

"I'll see to it," says Marica. "And I'll put up a sign that says, 'Do not enter. Water damage.' That should quell curiosity."

"Bless you," I say. It's a Nova Scotia expression, and it's spot on.

I'm disconnecting from the conversation, but something's rolling around in the back of my mind. I turn to Raynes, then Tiffany. "I have an idea, but it may not be a good one."

Both of them look at me, curious.

"I think I should call Zahra Bashir and invite her over." I turn to see what Raynes thinks of this. He may not be breathing. There isn't an eyebrow movement in sight. "My thinking goes like this. We give her advance notice of the news conference. She gets one night to broadcast ahead of the event, and we don't tell her much except the murderer has been caught."

"But why?" asks Raynes. "Why give her an edge?"

"I'm hoping it will give us an edge," I say to two perplexed faces. "If we're good to Bashir, maybe she'll be good to us." I see Raynes about to object, so I continue, "I don't expect preferential treatment or that she won't report on something, but Thorne always says media relations is more about relations than media."

"You could be right," says Tiffany. "When you know someone or owe someone, you see them in a different light."

We spend the next 20 minutes debating the idea and finally call Thorne. Whatever he recommends, we'll do. Thorne answers right away. In his world, Sunday morning calls are often disaster alerts.

We're not halfway through explaining our idea and its merits/demerits when Thorne says, "Oh for Christ's sake, invite the woman over for coffee. Tell her you have something that may be of interest, but make it clear she only gets what you are prepared to give her."

Well, that settles that. Almost. Raynes spends the next 20 minutes on the phone with his commanding officer explaining our plan. I'm sure the commanding officer spends the next 20 minutes talking to the police chief, but finally, it's agreed Bashir will receive an exclusive.

I make the call. Bashir picks up on the first ring. "I hate to interrupt your Sunday." I immediately am wondering if this is a sacred day for Muslims.

"Any time." Bashir sounds friendly, like the spider to the fly.

"I wanted to invite you to my house for a cup of coffee." I can feel both her confusion and her hesitation. "I'm here with Detective Raynes. And my wife."

"I'm on my way."

Tiffany takes something out of the freezer she calls peanut butter chocolate chip bars, but there is neither peanut butter nor chocolate chips in the recipe. I know that because I've eaten them before.

Raynes and I spend the next half hour planning what to say and do when the reporter arrives. We know it will all go to hell when she gets here, but it gives us the illusion of control. Bashir arrives around 10 o'clock, and she brings homemade banana bread.

"I thought we might want something to eat."

Tiffany laughs. "I thought the same thing." She holds out a plate of the faux dessert bars.

We're getting settled. Four cautious humans doing a polite dance. "Would you like coffee?" I ask.

"You should give her the poop stuff," says Raynes with a laugh.

"You have Kopi luwak?" Bashir turns to me with delight. "I've always wanted to have a cup. Or two."

Then again, who doesn't want to drink my $600-a-pound coffee, a gift from my wealthy father-in-law? I'm making the brew and thinking of ways to drop the cost into conversation with Raynes; hell, I may even charge him. Or maybe we can invoice this to the police department or my company. Now, we're talking.

The polite dance continues while the coffee brews in the press. Bashir is very complimentary about the dessert bars, so I'm on full alert for deceptiveness. Finally, coffee is poured, plates are pushed to the side, and the reporter leans in. "This is lovely, but I'm assuming this is more than a social call."

"We have an offer for you." I turn to Raynes for confirmation. He nods.

"Let's hear it."

"We will tell you something, and only you, but there are two conditions." I sense Bashir's uncertainty.

"I'm listening."

"The conditions are this. First, we will give you the information we can give at this time, and nothing more. We'd like you to accept that restriction. Second, we'd like you to keep your sources, that would be us, confidential."

"The second condition is easy," says Bashir, "and obvious." It sounds a bit like a challenge and a rebuke. "The first condition is not so straightforward. I will take the information you give me, but I may reach out to other sources to add or to confirm those facts."

Raynes and I exchange glances. We prepared for this. Time is running out though for Bashir to contact others and make it to air tonight, and it is Sunday. Also, aside from cops, who knows about this?

"Okay," I say, turning to Raynes. He takes the, well, you know.

"Tomorrow morning, the Halifax Police Department will hold a news conference to announce someone has been arrested for the murder of Norm Bedwell."

Bashir misses a beat. This was not expected. There is also a hint of glee. "Can you tell me whom?"

"No," says Raynes.

"Can you tell me if this was personal or professional?"

"No. But I can tell you we have a confession."

These points everyone has agreed can be revealed in advance of the news conference.

"Do you have permission from the Halifax police to share this information with me?"

"Does it matter?"

That seems to wrap it up. We can feel Bashir's energy and know she wants to move on this quickly. She thanked us for the treats, the information, and "the best coffee on the planet."

I walk her to the door. "Thank you. I have a feeling this was your idea."

"It was mutual," I assure her. "But it does mean I'll have to cancel our interview tomorrow."

I can see her scanning her calendar in her mind's eye. "Ahh, the leadership piece. How about we reschedule for Wednesday."

"That would probably work."

"It would have to be live."

That I don't like. "I'm fine with going live as long as the questions do not pertain to the Bedwell case."

"Deal."

I believe she means it. This exclusive is already paying off.

* * *

My afternoon fills with getting ready for tomorrow. First, I call our regulator, David Clements. He isn't thrilled about the news conference but relieved the case is closed and we can get back to business as usual.

"There will be questions about the romantic work relationship," he states. "Do you have a policy?" That's what has been rolling around in my mind since Raynes told me about the press briefing.

"We do not have a policy specific to romantic relationships, but we have a respect-in-the-workplace policy, which covers this." It doesn't seem enough. "Even if we had a policy specific to romantic relationships, it wouldn't matter. The very nature of an affair is that it is kept secret from everyone because it does break the rules of morality if not professionalism."

"I hope you're not speaking from experience." There is a hint of both frivolity and caution in Clements's voice.

"You've met Tiffany. I like breathing too much."

We end the call on an upbeat note. Not a hint of a "chunderfuck" anywhere. I really must find out what the hell that word means.

My father-in-law is also amenable to the plan Raynes and I have developed. I can see his throat slightly constrict when I mention we've given Bashir an exclusive, but this is nothing new for American politics. The media are routinely used as a credible conduit to send messages to voters and detractors.

"Sounds like you've got everything in hand." The senator hesitates, and I brace for criticism. I don't get any. Instead, he asks, "Are you okay?"

This is not expected. I'm unsure if John Williams is concerned for me, his daughter, or his company. And I'm certain that's fair on my part. This man might have a genuine affection for me since I've been part of his life for a decade. I must tactfully ask Tiffany how to interpret his question.

"I'm fine. No lingering aftereffects, except Tiffany squeezing me a little longer and harder. I can live with that."

"What you did is quite something. I'm proud of you, but please don't be that stupid again."

I promise to behave, and we hang up on that senatorial note. I'm starting to think this whole episode with Batshit may become part of my brand in the race for the Oval Office. American hero to the rescue, that sort of shit.

Wouldn't that be a chunderfuck?

Nope, still not right. I have to find out what the hell that word means.

Chapter 15

It's news conference day and I'm up at the crack of dawn. Tiffany already has breakfast ready. It's the yogurt and oats and blueberries thing with flax hidden somewhere inside. I'm sure its good for me. Maybe I can pick up a Timmy's sandwich on my way to work.

I'm swiping my card through the security gate when I see the light on in my office. Dammit, not another problem. I race up the stairs and down the hall, and see Marcia walk out my door. "Everything all right?" This is much too early for Marcia to be at work. She has a schedule and lives by it.

"Thought you might need a hand this morning," my secretary says calmly. "I have a sign up on Warrington's door, and I checked that the office is locked. The boardroom is ready. The video display is hooked up, and the coffee is in the machine, the Ethiopian blend you like. And I've ordered some danishes for the boardroom."

"In Norm's honor," I say, mostly to myself.

Marcia laughs. I grin, then stop. I hear Tiffany's voice inside my head, *"Have you forgotten anything?"* I turn to Marcia. "Thank you," I say. I mean it. "You are exceptional."

And for the first time, since I've known her, my 56-year-old executive assistant blushes.

* * *

The team is assembled and on full alert when I walk into the boardroom. It's one of those rare occasions when I am deliberately not early. The team received an email from me last evening before the 6 o'clock news, alerting them there would be an announcement, but I could not provide more information at this time. Most of them, I'm sure, have seen Zahra Bashir's report.

It was, as expected, devoid of details. Bashir announced the HPD would be holding a press conference to confirm someone had been apprehended for the death of Norm Bedwell. Bashir interviewed Neil Phillips, who intoned his traditional mantra about the evils of legalized cannabis, which fell flat beside Bashir's bombshell about the HPD arrest.

I get right to the point with the team. "Susan Warrington has been arrested for the murder of Norm Bedwell. She has confessed."

The room erupts. A thousand questions, many of them repetitive and rhetorical, are thrown my way. How long have you known? Why would Susan kill Norm? Are we all safe? Does Norm's family know? What will this mean for CCC?

We deal with the questions one at a time. That takes up roughly 45 minutes, but they are essential minutes. You can see the team adjusting to the news and reconciling it with their reality.

"I do have one more item. The news conference mentioned on the broadcast last night will start in 15 minutes. I thought we'd watch it together and identify any issues that we envision could arise."

Everyone looks at the clock. It's like we're counting down the minutes until 11 a.m. Or doomsday.

* * *

Raynes's division commander, Superintendent Leonard Morrison, starts the news conference promptly at 11. The time is strategic. It gives TV reporters time to conduct additional interviews and edit tapes before the evening news, but not too much time. Radio and online media will run with the story right away, which means, initially, coverage will be limited and stick closely to what is said at the briefing. The print will post something succinct online and run a more in-depth story in the morning.

It was decided yesterday that I should stay away. If I make an appearance, I'll get pummeled with questions and requests for an interview. Marcia is truthfully informing all reporters who call that I'm tied up in meetings all day; she has ensured I will be.

Faye Bedwell left yesterday with Bran to stay with her sister-in-law in Cape Breton to gain some distance between her and the media. Good move.

Morrison introduces himself as Superintendent of the Integrated Criminal Investigation Division and thanks the media for coming. He outlines the process for the news conference: he reads a prepared statement and then takes questions from the reporters. Following that, there's one hour allotted for individual interviews.

The Superintendent's comments are succinct and relevant. He's confident but approachable. I have no sense that he hides any information, no indication he offers more than necessary. Morrison tells reporters an arrest was made, and the individual has signed a confession. Motive is personal; there has been a relationship between the deceased and the killer, Susan Warrington, the director of human resources for the Canadian Cannabis Corp. The Halifax Police Department is officially closing the case.

My team knows more is coming, and I can feel their unease growing as Morrison nears the end of his statement. He flips the last page and turns to the camera. Almost simultaneously, the four men and women in my boardroom lean forward, and so do the reporters in the press room.

Morrison holds up his hand. "Before I open this briefing to questions, I would like to take a minute to express my sincere gratitude to the detective who oversaw this investigation, Detective Franklin Raynes. He has worked tirelessly to bring this case to a successful close and to bring some closure for Mr. Bedwell's family and friends."

Raynes is standing in full uniform over Morrison's left shoulder. He nods his acceptance of the praise, and the Superintendent moves out from behind the podium and walks over to Raynes. He extends his hand. It's a perfect photo op. I don't know if it is intentional.

The thank you is pro forma politics. What is unexpected is the sincerity of the gratitude. I'm also a little baffled by what is happening in my stomach and sternum. There is a pang of some kind, a small thrust to the gut, and a sensation of warmth. I wonder if I'm coming down with the flu.

Pro forma formally over, the media leans forward, each reporter eager to be the first to have their question answered. But Morrison, it seems, is not quite finished. "I have just one more comment. I know you're keen to get to questions, but this is important."

Now media are curious. So are all of us in the CCC boardroom. "Police work is often hampered by a reluctance for witnesses, colleagues, family, and others to come forward. To be forthright. In this case, we experienced just the opposite. On behalf of the Halifax Police Department, I would like to extend our official thanks to Riel Brava, chief executive officer of the Canadian Cannabis Corporation.

"From the outset, Mr. Brava has given us his full cooperation, opened his doors to us at all hours of the day and night without complaint, and encouraged his staff to support our investigation fully. He has gone above and beyond, offering ongoing assistance as requested and ensuring he was there to help at every turn. I understand that in his efforts to assist, Mr. Brava went so far as to eat his first donair, to the dismay of his wife, a vegetarian."

Morrison waits for the laughter to subside. It's not his first rodeo. His hand raises to quiet the crowd. "Donairs aside, Mr. Brava's assistance enabled Detective Raynes and his team to resolve the case very quickly and effectively. Thank you, Mr. Brava."

I am thunderstruck. So is my team. It wasn't on the agenda, not the agenda I was given. I look at my senior managers and shrug.

They stand up and applaud.

The stabbing in my gut and chest is back.

* * *

The rest of the day is a whirlwind. The executive team discusses the next steps: an email is drafted and sent to the employees within an hour, and Lucy Chen is reaching out to contract HR services until a replacement for Warrington can be found. That will be a very thorough search. I'll call the regulator. And the senator.

My first call, though, is to Raynes. It goes to voicemail, as expected. He'll be at the news conference or the subsequent debriefing. I thank him for the warm comments from the superintendent and for introducing me to donairs.

Before I can call the regulator, Marcia is in my office. Tiffany has been trying to reach me. I thank her and grab my cell. I realize Marcia is standing in front of me. "Everything all right?"

Without saying a word, Marcia walks toward me, stops, and wraps her arms around my waist for a quick hug. Then she turns and leaves.

It's going to be that kind of day. Tiffany is in tears when she answers the phone. I'm alarmed something is wrong. Apparently, she's proud of me. "Does that feel like a stabbing pain and a steam bath?" I ask.

She laughs. "It most definitely does."

"Does that mean I'm allowed the occasional donair?"

"It most definitely does not."

I hear a dial tone in my ear.

* * *

David Clements is expecting my call. He answers on the first ring, "I don't know how you do it, but shit does not stick to you."

"That 'thank you' was a complete surprise," I assure him. "I had no idea it was coming."

"I did. Detective Raynes called me yesterday to formally express gratitude from the Halifax Police Department for being a regulator that understands crimes are not always sector specific. That thank you will be put in writing."

I'm at a loss for words. Clements seems to think this is a natural reaction. I finally respond, "I'd say we can officially put this little chunderfuck to rest. It's over, and now, it's back to business as usual."

Calling Raynes is back on my to-do list. I owe him another thank you, but that call has to wait.

My call with the senator went much the same way as it did with the regulator. He's

308

pleased as punch. Clements obviously called him yesterday. My father-in-law knew what was coming and couldn't wait to let me know he was part of the inner circle. Tiffany also called her father following the news conference. By the time the senator and I connected, he'd already seen the video from this morning's media event.

"You came out of this smelling like a rose. I wasn't sure you would. It bodes well."

I want to continue the conversation. It bodes well for what? But now is not the time. I thank him for his advice and support. He can read between the lines. "Kiss my ... daughter," the senator says and signs off.

* * *

Tuesday is mine. The day starts with a refrigerated vegan granola thing that leaves you hungry for real food. I smile. It's familiar ground.

A stack of files and messages waits for me when I get to the office. I'm through most of them before the office is even half-full. This is progress. I feel my footing getting firmer. The rhythm of life returns to normal.

Marcia reminds me of my interview tomorrow with Zahra Bashir. I call Thorne to discuss strategy. We determine we don't need one. While the media reports Warrington's murder as front-page news or a lead broadcast item, the tenor is that of fait accompli. Thorne and I agree the item will be over and old by the time I show up in CCN's studio tomorrow.

Unexpectedly, Tiffany asks if she can come with me to the interview. I don't know whether to feel flattered or concerned. My wife and my work are usually separate entities. "I'd like to spend a little time with you," she says. "And I want to be sure there are no clandestine trips to the donair shop."

I know she is kidding. And not. Again, I remind myself what this whole ordeal must have felt like from Tiffany's perspective. I tell her I'm delighted she wants to come. We decide to make a night of it afterward and have dinner at a nice restaurant. I'm thinking barbecue ribs; she's thinking tofu. We compromise on fish.

I have another productive day in the office on Wednesday. Around 4 p.m. I head home to get Tiffany and change. Thorne and I agreed I should wear a suit but opt for a casual feel with a crewneck sweater under my jacket. By the time we're pulling into the CCN station on Robie Street, it's nearly 5:30. That gives us at least 30 minutes before the broadcast starts and likely another 20 before I'm on.

Bashir meets us at the front desk and gets us both settled with visitor passes. "Thanks for doing this. It sounds like you've had quite the week."

Tiffany squeezes my hand, and I smile. "Glad it's all behind us now." Indeed, it appears to have been in my rear view since the news conference on Monday. Only two media called, both smaller outlets, and we declined to speak as this was a police matter. And that's how reporters treated it. Our fear that this would be played as an "orgy in cannabis company" never materialized.

Bashir leads Tiffany to a guest area behind the cameras and explains she'll take me to the ready room to run through the live interview process and get me mic ready. Bashir is very pleasant and helpful. I wonder if this is the real person, the result of our exclusive, or a persona to lull me into a false sense of security. I am no longer relaxed. Bashir assures me, again, the interview will be straightforward. Now, I'm very worried.

When there are about five minutes to air, Bashir leads me down a back corridor to a stage set with three chairs and a coffee table. I raise an eyebrow, for the first time, at the additional chair, vigilant. Bashir shrugs my concern off. "Standard set layout. The camera angle will cut the third chair out of the shot."

Sure.

And we're live in ten, nine .... I see Tiffany out of the corner of my eye and smile. She waves. A tall grey-haired man in brown chinos and a crisp white shirt stands behind her. I turn toward Bashir as it strikes me that the man looks a little like my father-in-law. His presence, it appears, never leaves me.

Bashir dives in. She introduces the segment as the final installment in CCN Halifax's leadership series. She turns to me and offers a warm welcome. I smile, but I don't mean it.

"You're CEO of the largest cannabis production company in Atlantic Canada and the third largest in the country. This is a new sector. What challenges are you facing that are unique to the sector?"

This is as planned. We talk about running a new business in a new sector, anticipating consumer demand accurately, and ensuring we can meet it. It's a major issue for the industry. Once the novelty of legal cannabis faded, so did much of the public's desire to smoke weed, or even eat it. Once regular smokers saw the sticker price required to meet government standards, many returned to buying from their local neighborhood dealer.

Deftly, Bashir moves me away from my sector to the business needs of the city as a whole. I'm feeling confident in this territory. I sound knowledgeable; I sound like a leader. I know because Thorne and I have rehearsed this.

We're moving into wrap-up. Bashir glances down at her notes and back up at me. A smile lingers. Dammit.

"You've had an unusual and demanding week," the still-smiling reporter says.

Here it comes.

"We understand you were instrumental in successfully helping Halifax police conclude a difficult murder case."

I shift in my chair, a media training no-no. "All of us at CCC are relieved to see justice done and thankful to return to business as usual."

Bashir persists. "That's very modest of you." She pauses slightly. "According to the…" Bashir rechecks her notes, "Superintendent of the Integrated Criminal Investigation Division, you have gone above and beyond, offering ongoing assistance as requested and ensuring you were there to help at every turn."

I am distinctly uncomfortable and fear I am coming across as uncomfortable because I don't know where the hell she's going with this. "We see that as our collective role," I say. "It's my name that gets mentioned, but everyone at CCC who was asked for assistance gave it willingly."

Now Bashir is almost beaming. "That's kind of you to say. But we understand you willingly put yourself in harm's way to assist the police." I attempt to interject, but Bashir ignores my effort and continues, "We understand you were held at gunpoint by the killer."

Son of a bitch. Where did she get this? I'm frantically rerunning Thorne's training in my mind. I deflect. "The good news is that everybody and everything is fine. The killer is behind bars, and my vegetarian wife has forgiven me for eating a donair."

Bashir laughs.

I feel myself slowly unknotting.

"We have a surprise for you."

The knots tug harder.

The reporter is on her feet. I turn in her direction to see her shaking hands with a tall, casually but elegantly dressed Black man. He smiles in my direction. He's a dead man.

Lin Raynes turns toward me and extends his hand. His left eyebrow is arched, and a grin settles on his face. "On behalf of the Halifax Police Department and the City of Halifax, we would like to present you with the Medal of Bravery, extended to those who put the safety of others above their own."

I'm unaware of shaking hands with Raynes or him pinning the medal to my suit lapel. The newsroom erupts in applause. Tiffany and the grey-haired man are pushed toward the set. Tiffany hugs me and tries to hold back tears. The distinguished older gentleman comes in for a hug. At some point, I realize this guy is my damn father-in-law.

The rest of the interview is a blur. I'm sure it lasts only a few seconds, but I have no idea what I said, or anyone else said. I'm trying to sort out my state of mind and grasp how it unfolded without my knowledge.

Bashir deftly wraps up the segment, and we move to commercial. People are clasping my hand and patting me on the back. Raynes leans in. "Well deserved."

"I will get even." I look at him with a grin.

"We can discuss it over dinner." Of course, Raynes is invited to dine with us.

We're all leaving the studio, a happy and proud group. Raynes and Tiffany walk ahead of us.

I thank the senator for coming all this way. "It means a lot to Tiffany and me."

"It will also mean a lot to your political career. I can help you with that."

I'm stunned. That is an issue we have never discussed. Frankly, it's not ever been hinted at despite my ambitions.

The senator laughs. It's the laugh of someone who shares a deep, unbreakable connection with you. I have no idea where in the hell it's coming from, but for the first time since Norm Bedwell died, I am sure of one thing.

I know what "chunderfuck" means.

donalee Moulton is an award-winning freelance journalist who has written for print and online publications across North America including *The Globe and Mail, Chatelaine, Lawyer's Daily,* and the *National Post. Hung out to Die* is her first mystery book. Her short story "Swan Song" was one of 21 selected for publication in *Cold Canadian Crime* and a second short story has been published in *Black Cat Weekly.* donalee is the author of the new book *The Thong Principle: Saying What You Mean and Meaning What You Say,* and co-authored *Celebrity Court Cases*.